Top Shelf

Top Shelf

A McLaughlin Romance

Shelli Stevens

TULE
PUBLISHING

Dedication

Thanks to Jon Beach from Fiddler's, the fabulous restaurant I discovered in Drumnadrochit, Loch Ness, Scotland. Your patience and humor in helping me with my first whisky tasting was greatly appreciated. Thanks to TJ Goodman for all your help with Navy-related research, and to Sandy Rodriguez for introducing us! A huge thank you and virtual hug to my readers, and to Tule Publishing for giving this story a new home.

Chapter One

"I HATE THIS FUCKING rain, Chief."

Brett Craven had been so determined to get the hell out of the crowded hangar he hadn't realized Petty Officer Simmons had been quick on his heels. He arched a brow at the younger man.

The sailor ducked his head and flushed slightly. "Err, sorry about the language."

"Don't worry about it. And yes, the weather can be a little moody this time of year up here."

There was something to be said about being back in the cool drizzle of the Pacific Northwest. Maybe it was usually the locals who bragged about their love for this kind of gray weather, but even though he was a born-and-bred Southern boy, Brett realized it had grown on him. Then again, six months on an aircraft carrier in the Gulf Coast could make a person miss the small things. Like the stinging caress of a raindrop on your bare arm or the frigid breeze chilling your nose. The feel of a woman.

"You've only been at NAS Whidbey, what, a year, Simmons? Not to mention you've been at sea for half that. Give it some time."

"I'll never get used to it, Chief," the sailor, probably no older than twenty-two, grumbled.

It was easy to say that now what with winter in full swing. Everyone onboard the ship had recently rung in the New Year together. To Brett, it was just another holiday. One of many since summer that they'd celebrated without family. Loved ones.

It wasn't a new experience for him and, truthfully, it barely fazed him anymore. He wasn't one of the sailors missing a spouse and kids at home. Wherever home happened to be that year.

His chest tightened a bit and he drew in another lungful of cold, damp air. Once he'd had a wife he'd looked forward to returning to, but that had only lasted a couple years. Now it seemed like a blip on the radar of the almost two decades he'd served in the Navy.

"I'm going to put in for Hawaii next orders," Simmons muttered.

"Good luck. Remind me, you're from Arizona?"

"Yeah, and I sure do miss the heat. You can understand that—you're from Louisiana, right?"

"Sure am. New Orleans."

"You miss it?"

"Not as much as I miss Whidbey each time I get relocated, honestly."

Three of his orders he'd been fortunate enough to get stationed here on the island. With him coming up on retirement, he hoped these would be his last orders. He planned to stick around.

Brett cast another glance at the petty officer. "Why are you leaving the homecoming early?"

"No reason to hang around. I don't have a girl." Simmons shrugged and gave a lopsided smile. "But I intend to find one before the weekend is over. Bunch of the guys are going out to celebrate tonight."

Celebrate meaning pick up chicks. Try to get laid. Pretty common for the single guys returning home. Brett glanced back into the hangar, still crowded with people. Wives. Girlfriends. Husbands. Boyfriends. Children. Family. People who cared. It was the usual welcome-home gathering that tugged at the public's tear glands and brought the news media out to capture the event.

As much as he loved coming back from a deployment, this part was bittersweet for him. There was no wife to greet him. No children. Not even a girlfriend. That last one he had himself to blame for. Not that he wanted a girlfriend or even needed one. Well, maybe he needed one for certain reasons, but there were ways around that. Without the commitment and the risks.

"You should come out with us, Chief."

Though it wouldn't be the first time he'd gone out with his sailors, it was on the tip of his tongue to refuse. Nothing sounded better right now than heading home and pouring himself a glass of brandy, putting on some blues music, and appreciating the fact that he was back on solid land for a while.

"We're going to McLaughlin's Pub."

Just the mention of the Scottish pub on the island had the memory of *her* zinging through his mind. Kenzie. The pretty strawberry blonde with gorgeous green eyes who was a waitress at the pub. The night before he'd shipped out, he'd flirted with her, and while tentative, she'd seemed to flirt back.

Hmm. Six months on a boat and the possibility of seeing her again?

"What time are y'all heading over there? I'll try and drop by."

∽

KENZIE GRUNTED AND adjusted the massive box in her arms. She took a few more stumbling steps before depositing it— or dropping it—to the hardwood floors. She winced at the crunching of glass. Might need to buy new picture frames.

"Another box, another day closer to moving in," the ex-cited female voice quipped from behind her. "You need some help, *roomie?*"

Hands on her hips, Kenzie turned to grin at Delonna. "I think we're good. Aleck's right behind me bringing in another couple of boxes from his car."

"Nice. And you've brought me manual labor eye candy."

Kenzie gave a snort of laughter and again looked around the small rambler that Delonna had rented in Oak Harbor. It was cute, had two big bedrooms, a decent kitchen, and was close to her job at the pub. It was quite perfect for her really, but beyond the physicality of the house, she looked forward to the chance to finally make it out on her own. To step out from her family's shadow.

Not that she didn't love them to bits, but at a year shy of thirty, it was time she lived with someone besides a family member. She'd lived with her parents until they'd returned to Edinburgh several years ago, and then had rented a room from her oldest brother Aleck.

When Delonna's offer had come in she'd already been surfing roommate ads because she couldn't afford a place on her own while going to school and working as a waitress at the pub.

"Seriously, Kenz, you're saving my ass here by moving in. I was in major need of someone to pick up half the rent now that Jeanine bailed to live with her boyfriend."

"I still maintain you're doing *me* the favor. And that was totally shitty of her, by the way."

"Sorry, what was totally shitty?" a male voice asked from the doorway. "The fact that I'll now grow old, decrepit and alone in my house? Aye. Couldn't agree more."

Kenzie glanced back at her brother and rolled her eyes. "Oh please. At least bring balloons if you're going to throw yourself a pity party."

"Suck it up, buttercup." Delonna tossed her hair and took one of the boxes from him. "Think of it this way, now it's easier to put in that revolving door for all those women, right?"

"Oh, ouch, she has you there, my dear brother." Kenzie laughed and winked at Aleck.

He failed to look amused though and glowered at the two of them. "Hmm. I live the life of a humble monk—"

"Monk my arse." Kenzie snorted.

"—while the two of you as flatmates—"

"Roommates," Delonna corrected. "Try to remember you're an American now."

"—will get into all sorts of trouble and debauchery," he finished without acknowledging either of their remarks.

"Any debauchery I'm doing is with my boyfriend," Delonna murmured. "So I'm kind of harmless."

"Hmmm." If anything his expression darkened further.

"And that just leaves me." Kenzie had meant her reply to continue in the upbeat repartee, but it had a more deflated quality, like a balloon with a pinprick in it.

Debauchery and trouble weren't really her path. Not anymore, at least. Back in her late teen years, yes, maybe she'd been a bit more wild and flirty. After the incident everything had changed.

She'd gotten pretty good at pushing aside the dark memory, the fear, and she did so again now. Aleck seemed to dwell on it a bit more. The irritation in his gaze vanished, and it softened into sympathy.

Still, he played along. "And I'm sure I'll have to bail you out of jail more than once, aye?"

"Oh, aye," she agreed with a sardonic smile because they both knew it was complete shite. "At least once a month."

There was silence for a moment before Aleck scratched the back of his head and sighed.

"I think that's the last of it." He glanced over the boxes on the floor and dismay flickered in his eyes. "I still can't quite believe you've up and left the house."

"Your house," she replied softly. "I need a chance to go it on my own. Well, maybe not alone yet, but with someone who doesn't share my blood."

Aleck grunted, but didn't reply.

"Don't sweat it, boss boy. I'll keep her in line." Delonna's endearment came from the fact that she also worked at McLaughlin's Pub, which Aleck owned, as a bartender.

"I'll hold you to that." He met Delonna's gaze briefly before crossing the room and pulling Kenzie into a quick hug. "I'll miss you for certain, Sis."

Kenzie leaned in to the comforting embrace of her oldest brother and sighed. Aye, she adored this man.

"I know." She closed her eyes. "I'll miss you too, but for fuck's sake, we'll still work together, ya big baby."

"Exactly. She'll be fine," Delonna drawled. "You McLaughlins are super good at this overprotective shit, by the way."

Kenzie snorted. She didn't even know the half of it.

"All right. I'm off to work now." He patted her back and then pulled away. "Get yourself settled and let me know if you need anything."

"Will do. Love you, Aleck."

"Love you too, kid." Pausing at the door, he winked and turned to point a finger at Delonna. "You. Don't be late for work tomorrow."

Delonna's eyes widened with mock innocence. "Come on, really? I'm never late."

He arched a brow and stared at her until she cringed.

"Okay, maybe a few times. But I've gotten better."

With just a grunt as a reply, he disappeared from the house.

"I swear if your brother wasn't so hot, I'd wanna smack him upside the head some days."

Kenzie grimaced and shook her head. "You realize you both need to just fuck and be done with it."

Delonna gave a choked laugh. "Kenz!"

"Just saying."

"Well stop it and go find something cute to wear in one of those boxes."

"Um, any reason why?"

"Because tonight we celebrate a certain little birdie finally leaving the nest."

Seriously? She wanted to go out and party? Now? Kenzie

glanced around at all the boxes. "But I need to unpack. This place is a mess."

"The mess can wait. Go change."

Despite being bullied into it, Kenzie turned to walk down to her bedroom where an unopened suitcase sat. She hesitated and asked, "So where are we going?"

"Baxter's."

"Uh. That dive of a karaoke place?"

"Absolutely."

"Then you're absolutely buying my first drink." With a brief smile, Kenzie continued to her room.

∽

SHE WASN'T WORKING.

It was the first thing Brett had realized when he'd stepped foot inside the pub.

His gaze had immediately sought out a curvy strawberry blonde working the floor but hadn't found her. He'd found a cute African-American girl and a petite brunette, but no Kenzie.

Cradling his glass of brandy in his hand, he slid his gaze around the table and to the group of sailors he'd agreed to hang out with.

Maybe part of his reason for coming out tonight had been in hopes of finding Kenzie, but it wasn't easy to drop the leadership role, even on his day off. He was out to keep an eye on his sailors. Last time he'd been here one of his guys had been lucky not to get arrested after being a little too aggressive with a girl. Brett had ripped him a new one later. One thing outside of the military that he tried to pass on to these younger guys was that you treated women with respect.

His glance landed on Simmons, who was seated at the end of the table. A pretty blonde was perched on his knee, giggling and whispering something in his ear.

Simmons was drinking it in. His ears went pink at whatever she said and his arm tightened around her waist.

All the guys at this table tonight were looking for a girl. Some for just a night or two, others for something more serious.

"Let me buy you a shot, Chief."

Swinging his gaze to another of his sailors, he gave a short shake of his head.

"Thanks, Johnson, but I'm good with this."

"Ah come on, are you sure?"

"I'm sure."

His lips twitched as the sailor worked his way past the group and made his way to the bar. The few times he came out with his sailors it wasn't uncommon for them to try to get him drunk. It was a challenge. One they had yet to achieve.

No, he wasn't here to drink tonight. He'd been hoping for a different source of entertainment. Irritation and disappointment mingled. It was just his luck, really. He wasn't much into the bar scene, and the one night he did go out, hoping to find the one woman who'd sparked his interest in a while, she wasn't working.

When he'd seen her the night before he'd left it had been a Saturday night. She'd been working, so he'd assumed she'd be on again tonight. Maybe she didn't even work here anymore?

Biting back a sigh, Brett glanced at the bartenders behind the counter. One of the guys looked familiar. Maybe he could ask him?

Scooting back his chair, Brett made his way to the counter and waited for a break in the crowd of people ordering. Finally the guy he wanted to speak to turned his attention to Brett.

"What can I get you?" the tall, friendly looking man asked with what sounded like a Scottish accent. "Care for another brandy?"

"No, thanks, I'm good." He stepped closer to the counter. "I just wanted to ask if Kenzie still works here? When she works again?"

And just like that any friendliness vanished from the man's gaze.

"Kenzie, you say? Are you a friend of hers?"

Now how was he supposed to answer that? He couldn't really qualify them as friends.

"No, sir, not exactly."

"Then you'll understand if I don't exactly hand out that kind of information."

What the hell? That was a little extreme. Just what kind of relationship did this guy have with her? Were they a couple? The idea disappointed.

"Just what is your business with her?" the man asked, his gaze narrowed.

"Forget about it. Doesn't matter anyway." He tossed back the rest of his brandy and set the empty glass on the counter. "Thanks for your time."

Ignoring the answering grunt, Brett turned away and headed toward the door. It swung open a moment later. He barely noticed the first woman who strode in, but the flash behind her of hair that was more red than blonde had him pausing.

The first woman moved inside, straight to the counter, leaving the other woman exposed and standing alone in the doorway. His pulse slowed and then staggered into a slow gallop. Well, maybe his luck was about to change for the evening.

The other times he'd seen her she'd had her hair in a ponytail but tonight it fell in a long, loose curtain down her shoulders and back.

Her outfit, which could've easily been spotted on any guy in the room, was a U2 T-shirt and pair of skinny jeans, yet the combination was anything but masculine. The T-shirt was tight, clinging to large breasts and a narrowed waist. Her hips and ass were all rounded goodness and screamed blatant femininity in her dark jeans.

Brett blinked and had to unglue his tongue from the roof of his mouth.

Jesus, he hadn't remembered just how sexy she was. He'd known she was pretty, but this… Kenzie was a bombshell.

And he wasn't the only one noticing. One of his sailors appeared at her side, a stupid smile on his face as he said something to her. She gave a slight smile and shook her head before striding into the bar and walking behind the counter.

The man who Brett had just spoken to spotted her and grinned hugely, striding down to pull her into his arms and lift her off the ground. She laughed and kissed his cheek, slapping at his shoulders until he lowered her back to her feet.

Disappointment flared wide in his belly, and a brief flicker of jealousy that he hated to acknowledge. Well shit. Maybe they *were* a couple and that was why the guy had overreacted.

Kenzie pulled away from the man and poured herself a dark beer from the tap. Clearly she must still work here to take such liberties. With a wink at the men working behind the bar, all who watched her, she moved back out and onto the floor.

Brett hadn't meant to stick around like some skeevy gawker, but realized he hadn't moved when Kenzie nearly ran straight into him.

"Oof." She placed her hand out against his chest to stop the collision and offered him an apologetic smile. "Sorry about that, I didn't quite see you there."

Her gaze, just as vivid a green as he remembered, connected with his. The surprising wariness in her eyes slipped away to reveal confusion. With narrowed eyes, she tilted her head and studied him. Something about the way she did that was familiar.

"I know you," she said softly. "Don't I? Or do you just come here a lot?"

Amusement had a slow smile tugging at his lips. "Is that a line? Because if it is, it's not very original."

"A line? What?" Her confusion visibly increased and her scowl deepened. "No. It's not a line—I'm a waitress here."

"Hmm. Gotta say I'm a little disappointed it's not a line," he drawled slowly.

She folded her arms across her chest and stared at him, clearly trying to place exactly who he was. Maybe she wouldn't be able to. It had been six months and they really hadn't known each other. Just some brief flirting when he'd gotten her to promise to have dinner with him when he returned from deployment. Or, the deal was, so long as she didn't have a boyfriend.

He thought of the overly protective, grumpy asshole behind the counter who she'd just embraced. Clearly that dinner wasn't going to happen.

"You're right. I just come in here a lot, Kenzie."

He shouldn't have used her name, because unease flickered in her eyes and she took a step back.

"The hell you do. I'd remember you better. I know you from somewhere, but…ah shit." Realization dawned and her eyes went round. "You're that bloody sailor I promised to have dinner with."

With that last muttered statement, he heard the hint of an accent. The same accent as the bartender. Which just might mean he'd read the situation wrong.

"Is he related to you? The giant behind the bar?"

Kenzie followed his gaze. "Aleck? He's my brother."

Triumph seared through him and he arched a brow. "Is that so? Well, then. Yes. I *am* that sailor who you promised to have dinner with." He took a step toward her, not missing the slight hitch in her breathing. "And I thought I'd collect on that promise."

Chapter Two

H E REMEMBERED HER. How the hell had he remembered her?

Kenzie's heart hammered in her chest and she cast a panicked look around the pub. They hadn't even planned on coming here tonight, but Baxter's had been dead so they'd left after an hour to come have drinks and shoot some pool.

While he clearly remembered who she was, it had taken a moment for her to remember who *he* was. Working as a waitress here, she saw many people come and go. Many faces that became familiar. So many regulars who'd become close friends.

But he'd lied. This man, Brett was his name if she remembered correctly, wasn't a regular here. He'd only come in a handful of times that she knew of, and the two instances she could recall he'd made it a point to talk to her. Made his interest in her known.

Why had she been stupid enough to promise him dinner? It had been an impulsive response to his flirting when she'd been half-drunk at Sarah's bachelorette party. She hadn't for one moment thought he'd take her up on it.

It had been the night before he was going out on the ship for six months, he'd said. He'd been cute. Charming. Some kind of sexy Southern accent that had her pulse doing weird things, so she'd said yes. Had momentarily let down all the walls she had up around her heart, and said yes.

Who could've known he'd remember her? Taken her seriously even? But there was a stipulation. She only had to go out to dinner with him if she were still single.

From beneath her lashes, she ran a slow glance over him. While he'd called Aleck a giant, he certainly wasn't far behind. Likely several inches over six feet, he towered over her five-foot-six frame. His body seemed to be all muscle. He wore jeans and a nice button-up black shirt that showed the wide, hard-looking chest beneath.

She lifted her gaze from his chest and glanced over his shaved head, the small amount of hair there hinting the shade was probably a dark blond. Her attention fell again, as if drawn by an invisible beam, to meet his eyes. He watched her with a pale blue gaze that was so intense it became a struggle to breathe normally.

Shite, but he was attractive. A little too sexy, too confident, and the effect was enough to put her at unease. She drew in an unsteady breath and offered a small shrug.

"Dinner sounds lovely and all, but I'm actually seeing someone."

It wasn't a total lie. She was seeing someone. His name

was Benedict Cumberbatch and she saw him on her television once a week.

Brett stared at her through hooded eyes. She had the feeling he was scrutinizing her words for truth, but as far as he knew, why would she have a reason to lie? She very well could have a boyfriend as far as he knew.

"Bullshit."

Her breath caught. "Excuse me?"

"I'm calling bullshit on you having a boyfriend."

Bristling now, she straightened to her full height. "I find it a bit insulting that you'd doubt my relationship status."

"This isn't Facebook, and that's not what I'm doubting. Look, Kenzie, I came in here tonight to see you. I'm not going to lie. Six months ago I thought you were cute. Funny. Sassy. You intrigued me and that doesn't happen a lot."

He shook his head and disappointment flickered in his eyes. Disappointment in her, she sensed. Guilt swept through her, and a hint of shame. This man served in the military and risked his life for his country. For the freedom she was fortunate enough to have, and she was treating him like a pesky fly she wished to swat away.

She could feel her ears warming and she bit the inside of her cheek as she tore her gaze from him.

What was wrong with her? Why couldn't she be like a normal girl and just flirt? He seemed like a decent guy, one who was blatantly interested in her. She'd even promised to have dinner with him, and yet she was pushing him away.

She always pushed men away.

"Everything all right here?"

Kenzie flinched at Aleck's arrival. Usually she'd welcome his interference if a guy was getting too aggressive, but Brett wasn't really being aggressive. More just confident in a nonthreatening way. He was simply attempting to cash in on an offer she'd made.

Shite she sucked.

Aleck stepped between her and Brett, and the warning vibe radiated off him in spades. Usually his height and stoic presence could be intimidating to the scariest of men, but Brett didn't even flinch. If anything he just appeared irritated if not completely unfazed.

Something told her this was a man who was used to giving orders, not taking them. Being the intimidator, not the intimidated.

"Everything is fine, Aleck." Her words were quiet and firm as she kept her gaze on Brett. "I've got this."

"Aye? Well I'll not be too far away if you need me, luv." With another hard warning glance at Brett, he disappeared back behind the bar.

"Nice protective brother you've got there."

She struggled to explain, but there really wasn't any way to without getting into deep, dark subjects. "Look, he means well."

"I don't disagree. Actually, I think it's a good thing." He smiled slightly. "I have a younger sister who I'd give my life to protect. I get it."

And he did, she recognized that in his somber gaze.

"Clearly things have changed since the night before I left for deployment. Or I misread the signals. Either way, I'll stop bothering you and let you get on with your evening. Have a good night, ma'am."

He nodded and turned to leave. Her heart pinched. She didn't want him to leave, even if fear of the unknown was making *her* want to bolt.

"Wait, Brett," she blurted, grabbing his arm. "About those signals. You didn't misread them."

SERIOUSLY? WAS SHE for real? What the hell was going on in this woman's mind right now?

Frozen in midstride, Brett hesitated before turning around to face Kenzie again. He was torn between frustration and anticipation. Despite her statement that he hadn't misread her signals, she was a mass of mixed ones. At one moment seeming as if she were about to flirt, maybe even dipping her toes into it, and then backing off quickly the next.

Why the hell he wasn't halfway to his truck right now, he couldn't say for sure. High-maintenance women who didn't know what they wanted were definitely not his thing. He'd been there. Done that. So why was he getting all twisted up by a curvy ginger who couldn't decide what she wanted?

"Look, no matter how tempted I am to stay here and let you play your head games, I think I'd better pass." He shoved his hands into his jeans pockets and sighed.

He wasn't stupid. Sometimes it was better to cut your losses and walk.

"I've been on a boat for the good part of six months, flew home from San Diego just a few hours ago, and now, if you'll excuse my language, I'm pretty fucking tired."

She didn't even flinch at his words, a good indication that swearing didn't faze her. But guilt flashed across her face, followed by what seemed to be a mix of fear and desperation.

"No, please, don't leave. I *was* attracted to you that night."

He made a soft laugh of amusement, yet wasn't really humored. "That night, but not anymore?"

Her mouth opened and she started to reply, but then she drew her bottom lip between her teeth and nibbled. The blush of color staining her cheeks and the way her lashes fluttered made him think that, yeah, she was still pretty damn interested despite the weird runaround she was giving him.

This close to her, he could smell the soft, clean scent of her soap. No heavy perfume. If he were to slide his fingers into her beautiful red hair would it be as soft as he imagined? Would it hold the faint smell of her shampoo?

He wanted to find out. God, he'd been way too long without a woman. He had to curl his fingers into fists to restrain the natural instinct to touch her.

Despite what may have been an attempt to hide it in that gender-neutral outfit, every part of her body was exaggerated in the female form. It was hard not to physically respond to it. There were a handful of women in this pub tonight who would've eagerly taken him home with them, or let him grope them in a darkened corner.

But none of them had tempted him, and he rarely worked that way. He liked sex. A lot. He was your average red-blooded man in his thirties, added to the fact he'd been on a boat for six months and his only source of pleasure had been from his hand. So, yeah, it was a little hard to not think about what Kenzie would look like flat on her back on his bed.

That hair spread out on his pillow, those breasts freed from her shirt and bra. What color were her nipples? Pink? Red? Maybe a—

"Let me take you to dinner." Her bold statement shocked him out of his dirty thoughts.

Ah shit. He'd gone full-on triple X in his head while standing in the middle of a pub. Had it been obvious? Did he look like a guy seconds away from whipping his dick out and stroking off?

And you're a perverted fuck who needs to focus on what the object of your lust just said.

"You want to take me to dinner?" He repeated it, even though he was pretty damn sure he'd heard her right. It was a bit blindsiding after being given the runaround.

"I do." She lifted her chin and seemed to reach some kind of decision.

"You want to take me to dinner *tonight*?"

"Yeah. I guess it's, um, kind of late. Have you eaten?"

It was nearly ten, of course he'd eaten.

"Doesn't matter, I can always eat more. You sure about this?"

"Yes. Only… I don't want to stay here." She shoved fingers through her hair, sending the reddish strands back behind a delicately curved ear. "Why don't we go to Applebee's?"

Applebee's. It was bright, inconspicuous, but most of all it was a safe choice. Which he guessed was why she chose it.

"What about your friend?" He nodded to the blonde who was chatting up Aleck behind the counter.

"Delonna?" She followed his gaze. "I think she'll be cool with it. I'll go let her know, though."

"Great. I'll wait here and then we can drive over there."

She had started to move away and paused. "Actually, if you don't mind, I'd prefer to drive myself. Can we meet?"

Either she was about to blow him off in a big way, or she was really big on this safety thing. Despite her jittery behavior from the evening, he suspected the latter.

"Sure."

There was something different about Kenzie. He couldn't put his finger on it, but he had to ask himself why he was putting in this much effort. She moved past him and his gaze fell to the pert roundness of her ass swinging as she moved through the crowd.

All right, maybe it was kind of a no-brainer.

With the blood in his body stirring south, he grabbed his keys and headed out the door.

⁖

"YOU'RE SERIOUSLY ABOUT to go out with that Navy guy?"

After seeing the blatant shock on Delonna's face, Kenzie shifted and folded her arms beneath her breasts.

"Yeah. I am. I know it's a bit crazy—"

"It's not crazy, it's about time." Delonna squeezed her shoulder and sighed. "You need to get out there. Like seriously."

"I've been out there."

"Your last boyfriend was what, like, 1980?"

"Yes. I dated extensively while I was a twinkle in my father's eye," Kenzie drawled. "I need to go—I'm supposed to meet him at Applebee's. He probably assumes I've blown him off by now."

"He's probably hoping you'll just blow him period. And really? Applebee's?"

"It's a neutral spot."

"It's practical, pretty boring, but safe. It works for you."

Delonna waved her away. "Go. I won't tell your brother."

"And I appreciate that." She glanced at her brother who was busy making drinks. "He'll definitely not be thrilled."

"Another reason you're doing this dinner thing somewhere else?"

"Yeah." Kenzie turned to walk toward the door, adding, "And the kitchen here at the pub is closed."

"Wait, let me walk you out. I just need to grab my coat. I threw it behind the counter."

Kenzie was used to the gesture and didn't protest, even if lately she was starting to think it a bit silly. It was habit to anyone who knew her, knew what had nearly happened to her, to not let her walk out to her car alone at night.

"Fine. I'll meet you out front, Delonna. I need some air."

She stepped out of the crowded pub and into the darkness. She wasn't alone: a handful of smokers lingered nearby since it was illegal to smoke inside the pub.

Leaning against the side of the building, she let her gaze sweep around the parking lot. The pub had a light on the side of the building, and a streetlight nearby, but there were shadows. Especially back by the trees.

The trees.

Maybe it was because it had happened on a winter's night just like this, but this time when the memory rushed her hard she couldn't quite hold it back.

"YOU WANT ANOTHER drink?"

Kenzie hesitated to answer the man beside her as they walked toward the trees at the edge of the parking lot of McLaughlin's Pub.

She wasn't exactly a novice at drinking, but that would make three swigs from the flask of vodka. Not to mention he'd poured some in her soda while they'd grabbed a free dinner inside her family's pub.

If Da had realized that she'd been drinking under his nose at the pub, he would've had kittens.

It wasn't that she didn't drink—it was pretty common for when she was visiting family in Scotland—but she was still considered underage by almost a couple years here in America.

"I've had enough. Thank you." She had a good buzz and was at that stage where one more drink would topple her over into the drunk category.

From beneath her lashes she glanced up at the man beside her. Charles was beautiful. Maybe it was a silly way to describe a man, but he was. His blond hair was perfect. Not too long, but not short. And his eyes were such a lovely, striking shade of dark blue. She'd asked him once if they were contacts, but he'd sworn they were genetic.

Which made sense, because she'd seen pictures of his dad—a well-known judge on the island—and he had the same eyes.

"You are such a beautiful girl, Kenzie."

Flattered, she gave him a slow smile and tossed her long red hair over her shoulder.

"You think so? You're pretty handsome yourself, Mr. Charles Richland."

He winked and reached out to hold her hand as he led her beneath a tree. The sun had set in the past half hour and a chill swept through her.

She knew why he'd brought her out here. To have some fun without the prying eyes of her family. Not that they could've stayed; the pub was switching over to the twenty-one and up crowd and she'd had to leave. She knew the rules.

So she'd taken him up on his suggestion to go outside and walk around, knowing it was pretty much a chance to take it to the making-out level with him.

And truthfully she was a little excited for it.

She wasn't inexperienced; she'd dated and had a couple boyfriends. She was often told how pretty she was, especially when her body had begun developing early and her curves came in big time. Her virginity had left the building somewhere in her sophomore year of high school.

But Charles was different. He was a twenty-five-year-old man climbing the social ladder in life. Rich. Handsome. Many women chased after him, and yet he'd turned his interest her way.

"I've been waiting all night to get you alone, baby."

He grabbed her around the waist, pulling her hard

against him. His lips smashed down on hers, his tongue thrusting so deep she almost gagged.

When she finally escaped to grab some air, she was almost unnerved, but she took a deep breath and gave a shaky smile. She couldn't blow this. Couldn't afford to look like a nervous, immature girl who wasn't even twenty yet.

"That was nice. We make a cute couple, don't you think?" she asked, looping her arms around his neck.

"Couple? You got the wrong idea, baby. I already have a girlfriend in law school." He nuzzled her neck and slid a hand up beneath her thin sweater to squeeze her breast painfully. "Thought I'd just fuck you a couple times for fun. It's about time I tried a piece of this sexy Scottish ass I've heard so much about."

What the hell? Had he truly said such complete shite? He had a girlfriend? Was hoping to sleep with her and toss her aside?

She blinked, fury spreading through her, and unwrapped her arms from his neck.

"Aye, well I think I've changed my mind. Perverted, cheating narcissists aren't my type."

Rage killing her buzz, she turned and walked away, but the hand that grabbed her hair jerked her back so hard tears sprang to her eyes.

She stumbled in her heels, falling back against him and crying out with fury.

"Let me go, you bloody—"

His hand slapped across her cheek, sending her head brutally to the side. The move wasn't hard enough to leave a mark, but shocking enough to stun and incapacitate her for a moment.

And he took that instant to push her to the ground, hands everywhere, as he tried to push her skirt up above her waist.

She clawed, fought, screamed against the hand over her mouth, even as part of her wanted to deny what was about to happen. It couldn't. She wouldn't let it. Terror and adrenaline kicked in and she fought blindly with the instinct to get away. She may as well have been a mosquito up against a bear, and her fear only seemed to fuel his arousal. His strength.

Everything went hazy and dark for a moment as she retreated into herself mentally. She was brought back into reality when someone lifted her up off the ground.

It was her brother Ian, and before he rushed her into the pub, she was vaguely aware of Charles's body lying bloody and lifeless on the ground.

Her head had been spinning. She'd been in such distress and shock that even with the relief of her family rushing to her side, her stomach heaved up all the vodka she'd drunk.

With questions being fired at her, the police being called, she curled up on the floor and faded into the darkness.

"IT'S FUCKING FREEZING out here."

At the sharp words, Kenzie blinked from her thoughts and glanced up to see Delonna stepping out of the bar.

"Hey, you okay? You look upset."

"I'm fine," Kenzie said quickly, shoving her hands in the pockets of her jeans. "Just a bit hungry. I've not eaten since before we left the house this afternoon."

"Ah, yeah, seriously. I'm going to head back into the kitchen once you head out. See if there's any meat pies left from the dinner special." Delonna glanced her way. "So this sailor guy."

"Brett."

"Okay. Brett. You realize he's not going out to meet you tonight just for the food, right?"

"I know." Kenzie's stomach did a little flip as she imagined exactly what Brett was probably after tonight. "It's not likely he's going to get it. From me at least."

Reaching her car, she turned and gave Delonna a swift hug. "Thank you, sweets. If I don't text you by midnight, call the police."

"I'm pretty sure you'll be fine."

"Me too. I'll be home tonight."

Delonna arched a brow and pursed her lips. "You don't need to, you know. You could go have fun."

"I could, aye." After climbing into her car she started the ignition.

"But you won't, Miss I-Belong-in-a-Convent."

"The nuns wouldn't have me. I fuckin' swear too much."
Kenzie gave her friend the finger and then shut the door. As
she drove off, she glanced in the mirror and watched Delonna walk back inside, clearly laughing.

And this was why they would work well as roommates.

By the time she arrived at the restaurant, her stomach
was on spin cycle. She drew in a deep breath, trying to calm
her nerves, before climbing out of the car and walking into
the restaurant.

She spotted him immediately near the front, alone in a
booth with what looked like iced tea in front of him. His
gaze lifted then and landed on her. The scowl that had been
marring his face vanished as he stood and pulled out the
chair across from him for her.

"Wasn't sure if you'd changed your mind," he murmured.

Wincing with guilt she gave him an apologetic smile.
"Sorry. I got a bit delayed. I'll say that when I make a
commitment I generally keep it."

"It's a good quality to have."

She couldn't help but smile as he pushed her chair in.
"Tell me, Brett, would that be a Southern accent that
accompanies your charming manners?"

"It's actually faded some, but yes, ma'am."

Ma'am. Hmm. Did she attribute the formal address he'd
used several times to the military training or being raised a
Southern boy? Maybe a combo of both.

"Where are you from, Brett?"

"New Orleans up until the day I enlisted. How about you? I notice you've got yourself somewhat of an accent too. Scottish?"

"Aye. Edinburgh. Though I've actually lived more of my life in America than I did Scotland."

"Scotland would be amazing to visit."

"You've never been? I'm sure you've traveled extensively with the Navy."

"I've traveled a lot, yeah, but not necessarily the places you'd hit up as a tourist spot."

"Ah, that makes sense."

A waitress, an older woman who looked like someone's grandmother, appeared to take their order and Brett glanced at Kenzie.

"What'll you have to drink?"

She hesitated. With friends, she'd order a beer without missing a beat, but being this was the first time she'd been out alone with the man, she wasn't sure it was such a good idea.

"A Sprite would be great."

"All right." The waitress nodded. "Anything to eat?"

"Mozzarella sticks," Kenzie replied immediately.

She glanced at Brett, curious to see whether he'd be shocked or surprised. Amusement flickered in his eyes, but that was it.

"And an order of wings with the hottest sauce you have,"

he added.

The waitress nodded. "All right, I'll put that in for you guys and bring you your Sprite and another iced tea."

"Wings hmm?"

"I love them. I don't care how bad the sauce is that they put on it."

Well, there you had it. The man had a taste for crap food as well it seemed, but, shite, he must work it off fast. Again her gaze was drawn to the broad, muscled chest beneath his shirt.

Something stirred inside her. Interest and a mix of awareness in the opposite sex that she hadn't let herself feel in a long time.

"Why are you here with me, Brett?"

Mid-sip of his iced tea, he took a moment to swallow before setting his glass down.

"I told you back at the pub, but I'm happy to say it again."

"Right, no, you did tell me. I just…I don't get it. All right, so you think I'm pretty—"

"It goes beyond the looks."

She shrugged. "You don't really know me. How can you say that?"

"You're right. I don't. But even if I'd been blind and simply gone by the couple times we'd spoke, the sound of your laughter, I would've been drawn to you, Kenzie."

Despite her reluctance to be charmed, a little bit of

pleasure slipped into her bloodstream making her pulse skip faster and her head feel lighter.

"But surely you're looking for something more at this moment. I mean, there had to be a dozen women at the pub who were prettier than me, some with outstanding personalities to match, who would've taken you home in a heartbeat. You're dead sexy."

"Dead sexy?" The slow, pearly-white grin he gave in response only confirmed her dead sexy remark. "And what makes you think that's all I'm looking for?"

"Really?" She barely avoided rolling her eyes as she laughed. "Look, I'm not daft. You've just told me you were only recently off the ship. Surely you're looking to have sex. As are most of the sailors in the pub. Can you tell me, honestly, that you weren't hoping I'd go home with you tonight?"

He cradled his iced tea in his hand and stared at her over the rim of the glass. "No. I can't actually."

It was both a relief and a disappointment to hear it. If she were honest with him he might walk right out that door and want nothing to do with her after this. But half the reason she'd offered to take him to dinner was to give it to him straight. Help him realize what he was getting into if he were truly interested.

"I understand the whole having needs bit," she said carefully, "but I must be honest too. I don't move that fast. I'm not the sort of girl who simply goes home with a guy. I'm pretty careful with who I sleep with."

"That's respectable."

His words made her laugh silently. Somehow she'd become the respectable girl. A decade ago that would've been a joke.

"Thank you. I think."

The waitress returned with her drink and set another iced tea in front of Brett.

She took a sip of her soda, watching as Brett stirred in several packets of sugar.

"It's that Southern thing," he explained, "and y'all don't have sweet tea up here."

"Not really, no. I get it. I like my tea hot and sweet."

"Hot and sweet." He tilted his head and gave her a glance-over. "Now doesn't that just sound like a good description of you."

"Charming. I suppose I set myself up for that."

"As much as I'd like to take all the credit, you did."

Laughing despite herself, she shook her head. "Anyway, as I was saying, if you want to go find another more, um, accommodating woman after dinner, I won't be offended."

Okay, maybe she'd be a little disappointed, which was probably the most she'd let herself feel for a guy in forever.

Not wanting to dwell on that dismal realization, she waited for his reply.

Chapter Three

BRETT STARED AT the woman across from him. Despite her casual statement that he could go bang some other chick tonight and she wouldn't care, there was tension in her shoulders.

Damn, but if she wasn't the sexiest and most puzzling woman he'd ever met, and it was almost as if she didn't give a flying fig about being sexy or flirtatious.

Like what she was doing right now. The way she played with the straw in her soda, sliding her fingers up and down the plastic and stroking a finger over the top. He'd bet all the money in his wallet it was subconscious.

But whether subconscious or beautifully calculated, the gesture was so seductive all he could think about was her fingers doing the same damn thing on his dick.

Dragging his mind from his filthy hand-job vision, he tried to remember what he was supposed to be answering her about. Oh right. Her half-assed encouragement that maybe he might want to find another woman later if he wanted to get laid tonight.

The idea was so off-putting he couldn't help but give a soft, harsh laugh. No other woman was going to be able to substitute for Kenzie right now. He wasn't like one of his younger sailors who simply needed release and would take it with any willing woman.

He wanted to get off tonight, just as much as the next guy. But he got the feeling Kenzie would be worth the wait.

"I'm enjoying my time with you," he finally answered, "and I'm actually okay with the knowledge that you're not looking for sex tonight."

Skepticism flashed across her face. "Seriously? Because I know you guys have been holding off on the ship and you must be horny as hell."

While maybe she wasn't looking for sex tonight, she certainly didn't seem shy discussing it.

Deciding to see exactly how comfortable she was, he pushed it a little further.

"Well, yes, most of us probably *are* horny as hell, but while we may not be sleeping with our women, it doesn't mean we're not getting off."

Her cheeks filled with color, and her gaze with realization. "Oh. Oh right. I mean, I guess it's only natural taking care of business yourself. I mean, I do it."

Christ Almighty, he didn't need that visual right now. Sweat broke out on the back of his neck. He really didn't need to think about Kenzie in bed, with her fingers—

"So maybe you don't really miss sex all that much?" she

asked with a slight frown.

"Of course we miss it—frigging your hand is nothing compared to a flesh-and-blood woman." His voice was a rasp now. "Which is why we make sure we're ready to meet our women when we come home."

"What do you mean by ready? Or do I want to know?"

He leaned forward slightly and covered her hand with his. It was meant to be conspiring, but really he just wanted an excuse to touch her.

"You tell me, Kenzie, do you really want to know?"

She bit her lip, glancing at his hand and almost hesitating, but she didn't pull away. She gave a quick nod. "Aye. Tell me."

"BOCOD," he whispered.

"BOCOD? What's that?"

"Beating Off Cut-Off Date."

Her eyes rounded. "Shut up."

"No really, it's a thing."

"You, like, stop getting off so you guys have this pent-up frustration. Then you arrive home and go at it with your wives and girlfriends."

He grinned, amused by her response. "And boyfriends for some. Times are changing. But yeah."

"Wow." She bit her lip, her eyes dancing. "I love it."

Even though her delighted words were backed up by her relaxed body language, surprise slid through him.

"You do? Really?"

He traced a thumb over her knuckles, loving how soft the skin was. Luxuriating in the fact that he could finally touch her. Even in such a small, innocent way.

He heard the soft hitch in her breathing and her gaze never left his.

"Yeah. It's actually kind of sweet."

"Well, it's not sweet, it's hard as hell."

"No pun intended?"

"Actually, yes—" he glowered mockingly "—pun intended."

She laughed then. A loud, belly laugh that wasn't the slightest bit sexy or feminine. Several people turned to glance their way. He loved her laugh, in all its bawdy, unrestrained glory.

The waitress arrived with their food, setting it down on the table. Brett pulled his hand away reluctantly. It'd be a little weird trying to eat holding her hand. He'd gotten away with it in the moment, but something told him she would get skittish after too long.

"Anything else I can get you two?" the waitress asked, giving them both a knowing look.

"I think we're good." Brett smiled. "Thank you."

"Must be nice to have your man back, dearie," she said, winking at Kenzie. "Welcome home, sailor."

Kenzie froze, a mozzarella stick halfway to her mouth, her eyes wide.

"She must have assumed because we were getting along

so well," Brett assured her, reaching for a wing. "Don't look panicked."

"Aye, of course. It's just, it threw me off-balance for a moment," she muttered and took a bite.

"That makes two of us."

They ate the greasy food quietly for a moment. When he reached for his iced tea, she spoke again.

"One thing I've always loved about this island is how supportive most people are of the Navy. How warm and welcoming they are when you guys return from being deployed. Or how everyone pulls together when you leave."

"I agree. You find that in a lot of military towns." He gave her a curious glance. "You must see a lot of sailors and spouses come in and out of the pub. It's not far from the base."

"We see a good amount," she agreed. "We've seen several couples married after meeting at McLaughlin's."

"And I'm sure a good amount get divorced from too many nights there." The words were out with a bitter edge before he could stop them.

Her gaze swung to his, full of shock.

Shit. Why the hell hadn't he filtered himself?

"What do you mean?"

"Nothing." He shook his head and reached for another wing.

"No, it's quite clear you meant something, so maybe you should elaborate."

Her brows were drawn down into a frown and he knew she wasn't about to drop the subject.

"Only that sometimes married people end up cheating on their spouses after hanging out in the bars too much."

"Well that's complete shite. Those same unfaithful bastards might be as likely to cheat with someone they met at the local grocery."

"Not always the man cheating, sugar," he drawled. "Just as often, it's the woman."

"Hmm." She didn't look convinced, but maybe slightly irritated now. "Well, I'm not on ring patrol when I'm working at our pub."

He needed to change the subject. Fast. He latched on to something she'd said, partly because he wasn't sure he'd heard right.

"Did you say 'our pub'?"

"Aye. Well, it belongs to my brother, so technically it's his. But we consider it our family pub. My parents started it when they moved here."

"Your parents are the McLaughlins in McLaughlin's Pub?"

"One and the same. We're all McLaughlins."

"Well, I guess I should've put that one together. Kenzie McLaughlin." He drew out her name on his tongue. It was sexy. Cute.

Matched her to a T. She was fun and cute.

He watched as she pulled her drink forward and slid the

straw between full lips unadorned with gloss or lipstick.

She was also ridiculously sexy in a natural way.

The next hour passed just as easily as the first. Conversation flowed with ease, and below the safe discussions, there was simmering heat that built. He knew it couldn't be one-sided.

When the bill came he snatched it and paid, despite her protests and insistence that she'd offered to buy his dinner. His mother hadn't raised him to let a woman pay for dinner on a first date. Maybe down the road, if she threw a fit, but it was bred in him to pick up the check.

"May I walk you to your car, Kenzie?"

She only barely hesitated before she nodded.

Be a gentleman. He kept the mantra in his head as they left the restaurant.

A kiss on the cheek. He wouldn't push her.

But his blood was hot and pounding, and he curled his hands into fists, knowing it was going to be a lot harder than he fucking thought.

EVEN THOUGH SHE'D been sipping beverages all night, Kenzie's mouth was dry as sandpaper.

Her heart beat a frantic rhythm as she walked beside Brett to her car. She'd successfully made it through dinner with him. A date. Technically it had been a date, right?

And now the evening was coming to a close. That point

where he might go in for a kiss. Might try and do some petting if she gave him any encouragement.

A wash of cold swept over her, mingling with the heat in her blood.

Oh God. She wasn't ready for this. Was she?

She could've told him she'd walk out to her car by herself. They were by a busy street and it was light enough. She would've been fine.

But she hadn't wanted to go out alone, and not because of fear, but because surprisingly she didn't want this night to end. It had been both terrifying to realize, and a bit liberating.

She was all too aware of his tall, wide frame walking beside her. Just how blatantly large and male he was. She was used to her brothers, but they were family. Brett was most definitely *not* a relative, and each step she took toward her car reminded her of it.

She reached her destination and drew in an unsteady breath.

"Here's my little Escort." She tried for a bright smile, but it felt tight. Fake. *Terrified.*

He stopped beside her, inches away, and didn't say anything. She could feel his gaze on her. Probing. Questioning. Heated. She'd seen that flash of need in his eyes more than once inside the restaurant, but he'd been a perfect gentleman. Doing nothing more than touching her hand briefly.

She'd been almost disappointed when he'd moved his

hand away. Would he try and touch her again now?

Her heart doubled its rhythm and she drew in tiny shallow breaths as panic started to swell in her.

"Brett—"

"Relax, Kenzie," he said softly. "I'm not going back on my word. I'm not going to seduce you in the parking lot of Applebee's."

He wasn't? Maybe it was a bloody shame, because with the way her body was reacting right now, she sensed he might've succeeded further than any man in the past ten years had.

With a soft curse, he muttered, "I have to kiss you, though. Please don't say no."

Say no? Could she even if she tried? Yet giving any kind of permission was nearly as impossible at this moment.

She could only stand frozen, eyes wide and heart racing. Finally, she gave a small nod.

He drew in a ragged breath and reached out to cradle her cheek with one hand. His other rested on her waist.

"I hope that was giving me permission, sugar, because I need only a taste."

Without waiting for a response, he lowered his head and his lips hovered just above hers. She closed her eyes, letting her senses take over. Their breath met first. Warm and moist, their lips not quite touching yet. Then he moved ever so slightly so that his mouth pressed against hers. Soft, but firm.

There was restraint in the hand that held her waist. His fingers on her skin, even over the cotton of her T-shirt, seemed to brand his prints. Making her burn. His grasp was strong, but not imprisoning.

His lips brushed hers again, softly, without pressure. He made no move to deepen the kiss or rush anything. It was simple and yet so sensual. The warmth in her belly began to spread through her blood, bubbling hotter and faster. Making her aware of every nerve ending in her body, but everything homed in on the one spot where their breath mixed together.

She wanted more. She wanted to deepen the kiss.

For an instant, his thumb pressed harder against her waist, and she could sense him struggling with his control. His lips trembled against hers and then, in a surprising move, he caught her bottom lip between both of his and sucked lightly.

Shock and pleasure jolted through her, and she whimpered, swaying against him. She needed more. Her lips parted and she leaned forward, but he'd already pulled away.

Dazed, she blinked her eyes open. It took a moment for her vision to adjust to the streetlights that held the nighttime darkness at bay.

"Thank you for taking me to dinner, Kenzie," he murmured, tracing his fingers down her jawline, ever so lightly.

"You actually paid for it." Oh shite, her voice sounded like she'd swallowed a squeak toy. "Thank you."

He gave another smile, the one that had all those little butterflies coming to life in her stomach. In the artificial lighting, she could see the lingering heat in his gaze and something else. Some kind of hesitancy.

He truly wasn't going to try to convince her to go to bed with him tonight. That fact in combination with how amazing the evening had been was making it harder to find a reason to not want to see him again.

Brett was a good guy. And she needed to start dating. Delonna was right. She really, really needed to put her arse out there.

And that kiss…whoa.

"I work tomorrow night—you should come in and see me. I'll likely hook you up with some shepherd's pie."

Wow, that was quite bold of her, wasn't it? Channeling some vintage Kenzie, she was. Biting her lip to hide a smile, she reached into her purse for her keys.

"Sounds good. Have a good night, Kenzie."

"You too."

He was rather sweet, waiting until she'd climbed into her car and driven off. Only then did she see him in her rearview as he made his way to a big pickup truck in the corner of the lot.

This was good. She'd met a decent guy and he was the perfect person to jump feet-first back into the dating game with.

It didn't have to be serious. Honestly, she didn't know if

she even wanted serious while she finished up her degree.

But she was putting herself out there, and it was about time.

BRETT MANEUVERED HIS Dodge Ram into a spot at the pub. The place was already packed even though it was a Sunday night. Maybe because there was a Seahawks game on and McLaughlin's Pub had a couple massive flat-screens throughout.

It all sounded pretty awesome actually. The game, a couple beers, shepherd's pie and a beautiful girl he hadn't been able to stop thinking about.

He'd gone all out this afternoon. Taking an extra-long shower and finally opening his bottle of Marc Jacobs aftershave. It had been a gift from his sister at Christmas, sitting unused in his bathroom until today. Not much for designer things, he figured his under ten dollar bottle was absolutely fine and he'd hold off on the pricey stuff once he ran out.

But today he saw the appeal in the designer brand. Felt the difference. Actually, he figured he smelled pretty damn good right now. And getting dressed, hell, he hadn't put that much thought into what to wear since, well, maybe never.

To top it all off, he was nervous. Like he was about to go on some kind of first date in high school or something.

What the hell was wrong with him?

Staring at the front door of the pub, watching people slip

in and out for a cigarette, a sliver of unease raced down his neck.

He shifted his gaze to one of the windows of the pub, saw the crowds of people. Some clearly sailors from the base.

Just as suddenly, she filled his vision. She had a tray of food balanced on her hand as she delivered it to the table near the window. Her hair was always the first thing he noticed. It was as much her identity as the trace of a Scottish accent.

Even from across the parking lot, he could get a good glimpse of her. So beautiful. His pulse jacked up and he drew in an unsteady breath.

With the food delivered, she tucked the tray under her arm and placed a hand on her hip. She seemed to be talking to the men, but her gaze rose to the window.

Through the drizzling rain and fading light, he knew she wouldn't be able to see him.

She lingered for a moment more, staring out into the night, before turning and walking away.

Shit.

Realization hit with him quick, cold precision.

He liked her. He liked Kenzie in a way that meant he might not be able to sleep with her for a couple of weeks, or even a night, and move on.

How? They'd had two hours talking at Applebee's and a kiss that most would consider chaste, for fuck's sake.

He scrubbed a hand down his smooth, expensively scented jaw, and was reminded of how hard he was trying tonight.

The excitement of the evening slowly faded into the depths of somber disappointment. He couldn't go down this road, not again. Nothing serious.

It was a promise he'd made to himself after the last time and one he'd done damn well at keeping.

The women he'd gotten involved with in the past couple of years had known what they were getting into. It had been casual. It had been fun. It had been brief. It had never been permanent.

Kenzie wasn't the kind of woman you slept with and walked away from. She'd blatantly said last night she didn't move that fast getting sexually involved with men, and he'd been fine with that. He knew she would've been worth the wait.

But despite the light-hearted yet tough exterior she presented, he knew she was fragile. Delicate. Though he suspected she'd smack him one if she ever heard him call her that.

She'd been hurt before. By someone. Maybe she hadn't told him, but some things you could sense.

His chest tightened and his stomach roiled. The dejection lingered in a heavy cloud around him as Brett started his truck, the keys still in the ignition.

He couldn't do it. He couldn't be the man who hurt Kenzie again. It was better if he walked away now.

Reversing out of his spot, he sped out of the pub's parking lot and forced himself not to give it a backward glance.

Chapter Four

"SCHOOL'S OUT. I don't know how the heck I'm going to keep my sanity all summer long."

Sitting on the front porch of Sarah and Ian's house, Kenzie smiled slightly at Sarah's pained words. Her brothers were in the back grilling dinner while Kenzie and Sarah sat on the porch chatting. Unfortunately, Hailey hadn't been able to make it to the weekly family gathering because she'd been called in to work.

Kenzie stared at her niece, who was doing backward handsprings in the yard, and gave a small shrug.

"I'm sorry you can't use wine to help this time." Kenzie lifted her own glass and gestured to Sarah's baby belly. "Don't want to get my future nephew drunk, so I'll be sure to drink another glass for you."

"Aren't you wonderful," Sarah drawled, then sipped on her lemonade.

"I can't remember. Is this barbeque tonight celebrating that it's summer vacation? Or trying to distract from the pain that your child will be telling you how bored she is for the next two months?"

"I think a little of both." Sarah rubbed her belly. "Though I'm sure Auntie Kenzie will take her for a few dozen sleepovers, right? Please? Oh God, please say yes? I'm already exhausted from being pregnant."

Sarah was so tiny that she'd begun showing pretty quickly into the pregnancy. Now at six months she was already almost all belly. Emily was over the moon at the idea of being a big sister.

Kenzie laughed and shook her head. "You doubt me? Of course I will. I adore my niece."

"You spoil her rotten."

"I believe that's actually the definition of adore, isn't it?"

Sarah arched a brow.

"Aye, well it should be then." Kenzie sighed and leaned back in the chair.

Her gaze drifted out over the handful of houses in the distance and the road that led down to the quaint town of Coupeville. It was rather pretty. One of the oldest towns on the island and still with that small-town feel.

"You've been back here a year now—do you ever tire of island living?"

"Not at all. I love Whidbey." Sarah's expression turned whimsical. "It's beautiful and peaceful. When we moved to Japan for Dad's orders, I didn't just mourn leaving Ian, but the island too."

"But it must've been nice having been able to travel."

"You really don't have much choice if you're in the Navy life. I'm not much for moving around since I did it so much as a kid." Sarah grinned. "If you're thinking about traveling, you should go and marry yourself a nice Navy man and—oh *fuck*."

Kenzie's grimace deepened.

"Shit, Kenz, I'm sorry. I forgot for just a minute and completely let that slip."

To hear her friend dropping swear words left and right almost erased the slight stab of sadness that had bloomed at Sarah's Navy man remark.

"No need to apologize. Seriously. We had one dinner together, and I'm not even sure I'd call it a date." She forced a light shrug. "And it was seven months ago, so it's water under the bridge."

Seven months. Shite, that was over half a year. Why did it still bother her this much?

Sarah clenched her glass of wine in her hand, clearly distressed. "I know, but—"

"You don't need to tiptoe around the topic of the Navy or Navy men, for fuck's sake. We live on an island where there's a base nearby. They're sewn into our lives by nature."

"They are. You're absolutely right. But I try and be careful and not mention them, because you don't need to be reminded of a certain asshole sailor."

Certain sailor meaning Brett. This was why you didn't tell your friends all the little details about your love life. Or lack of a love life.

The night after she'd had dinner with Brett, she'd met Sarah, Delonna and Hailey for breakfast. They'd all inhaled four-digit-calorie meals while she'd scooped on all the details on Kenzie's first date in a long-arse time.

Real brilliant move there, because Sunday night Brett hadn't shown up at the pub. Actually, he'd pretty much avoided coming to the pub every night for the past seven months. Radio silence. He didn't have her number and she didn't have his. Not that she would've called him.

The ball had been in his court. He knew where she worked while she only knew he worked on a Navy base with about a zillion other people. Clearly, he'd dropped the ball. Then again, maybe he'd never wanted to have it in the first place.

Yet she'd been quite a fool and had held out hope for the next couple of weeks that maybe something had simply come up. Maybe he'd been called back on the ship. Did that happen?

Until she'd spotted him a few weeks later in the grocery, walking through an aisle with a pretty woman at his side. Kenzie had hightailed it out of the store in a heartbeat, leaving a cart full of groceries and the insensitive wanker behind.

It had all become clear, including how naïve she'd been. Brett had been indulging her at dinner that night, but obviously his pressing need to get shagged had been greater than waiting to see how long it would be until she put out.

"He's not necessarily an asshole, Sarah." Even as she said it, she wondered why she was defending him. No, she couldn't be that silly. "He was simply a horny sailor hoping for a bit of immediate fun. Seeing that I wasn't ready to give it to him, he obviously went elsewhere."

"Apparently," Sarah grumbled. "Well, I never met him, but he sounded like a nice guy from what you said and I was pretty excited to hear you were putting yourself out there and dating."

Kenzie didn't reply, but stared at her niece who continued to do flips on the lawn.

It really was better that her brothers hadn't realized she'd gone out on a date and then been stood up. To say they would've lost it would be an understatement. Aleck in particular, as he'd had a bit of a run-in with Brett that night.

Shite, what was she doing still thinking about this man? Giving him a minute of her thoughts? It was ages ago.

"Is there anyone out there who has caught your interest lately, Kenzie?"

Ah, the girls were always fishing for the latest on her love life. They'd calmed down for a couple months after Brett, giving her time to heal if she'd needed it, but then jumped right back on the train.

"I don't know if it's interest," she admitted slowly. "But there is someone."

Sarah jumped on it like a kid on cake. She sat up in her

chair and leaned forward. "Seriously? Spill the beans. I want details and I want them now."

"I met him at my gym. He's a trainer there."

"You go to a gym?" Sarah's eyes widened ever farther. "And *you use a trainer*? But you hate exercise."

"I don't bloody hate exercise, I hate sweating. There's a difference, and shouldn't you just be excited I've met someone?"

"I am. Oh, absolutely. Is he cute?"

"He's attractive. Maybe a little unconventional. Loads of hair that he keeps in a ponytail—"

"Wait, you like long hair on guys?"

"—and I don't believe he has an inch of fat on him," she continued, ignoring the dubious look from her friend. "He's big and wide—"

"So are semi-trucks. Keep going. Does he have a good personality? Do you guys have much in common?"

"Well, we both like to work out."

"But you don't like—fine, you don't like to *sweat*. What else does he have going for him?"

"I don't know, Sarah, it's early. We've only talked in the gym and mostly about fitness stuff." She paused to take a sip of wine. "He's a single father—he told me that much. Has a son who's three."

"Oh wow. A kid, huh? But you do love children."

"Do I?" Kenzie shook her head and frowned. "Sometimes I wonder if I just prefer borrowing other people's.

Maybe the most I'm supposed to be is an aunt."

"Please. You've got plenty of time to decide."

"I'm almost twenty-nine," Kenzie pointed out.

Sarah shook her head in dismay. "You realize people do get pregnant past thirty, right? Do we need to talk about how babies are made?"

"Sausage goes in the crescent roll, something of the sort."

"Sausage in the crescent roll? Well. That's a new one."

"Thank you." She lifted her wineglass and winked. "I try to stay cutting-edge with my perverted analogies. Regardless, I know how babies are made. Even if I haven't participated in anything quite that fun lately."

Sarah gave her a pointed glance. "Well maybe this trainer guy is exactly what you need then."

Even as the thought of sleeping with the man did absolutely nothing to her pulse, she still gave a small nod. "Maybe. We're having dinner at Fliers tomorrow night."

The front door swung open and they both glanced back to see Ian strolling out.

"Dinner's about ready. You gals coming?"

"I'm hungry enough to eat my arm off, so aye, I'm coming." She nudged her brother in the side. "Took you long enough."

Ducking under him before he could get her in a head-lock, she slipped past him and down the stairs of the porch. She glanced back with a laugh, but it faded. Ian had already changed his course and helped his pregnant wife to her feet, planting a tender kiss on Sarah's lips.

Feeling a bit intrusive on the tender moment, she turned her attention away and sought out her niece to let her know it was time to come to dinner.

"WHAT ARE YOU having next, Chief? This one's on me."

Brett grimaced and set down his now empty pint. If he had a *next one* he'd be getting a little too close to being buzzed. Something he prided himself on was always being sober around his sailors. Even if a good amount of them were considered friends, he still had an image to uphold.

Tonight was just going to have to be another missed opportunity to get their chief drunk.

"I'm good. Thanks, Roberts."

"But it's your birthday, and you don't turn thirty-five every day, Chief," one of the guys across the table pointed out. "Come on, one of us can make sure you get home okay."

Thirty-five. Hell, how had he gotten so old? Only three years until retirement. It sounded unbelievably close, and yet felt like dozens of years away.

Even if he'd preferred to hang out at his house and catch the baseball game alone, he couldn't turn down his overeager sailors, most he considered friends, who'd insisted on buying him dinner and beers. Well, two beers. He was cutting himself off.

"I'm switching to water. Thanks, though."

The table of men grumbled good-naturedly but didn't slow their drinking. Which was another reason Brett kept his ass sober. Someone needed to keep an eye on these guys and make sure the designated didn't drink.

Since they were in a restaurant brewery type place, the designated was the poor nineteen-year-old who was old enough to die for his country but not old enough to have a beer.

But the boy took it in stride, keeping up with the conversation and seeming to enjoy every moment of the evening. Besides, Brett didn't doubt for one moment the young sailor found ways to drink outside of the bar situation.

"Holy shit. It's Petersburg," one of the guys muttered.

"Petersburg?" Brett scratched his memory, and came up with the sailor who'd discharged honorably out of the Navy last year.

A quick glance behind him showed the familiar guy standing at the hostess area of the crowded restaurant. Same features, except he'd grown his hair out long.

"He'll be waiting a while for a table with that other party over there taking up half the restaurant," Roberts pointed out. "We got room here since a couple of our guys took off. You all cool if I invite him to chill with us?"

"No problem at all," Brett drawled and pushed his beer aside to reach for the water. It'd be nice if their food arrived soon.

"Shit, Petersburg isn't alone. Do you see who his date is?

It's her. That totally hot chick."

"Dude, yeah, isn't she that hot waitress?"

Ignoring his sailors' discussion about Petersburg's apparently hot date, Brett just shook his head.

"Yeah, the one from McLaughlin's Pub."

Wait, what? That caught his attention. Swiveling in his chair he slid his narrowed gaze beyond Petersburg. He hadn't seen her at first because she'd been standing directly behind him, but now that the former sailor was heading their way, she was following and in no way hidden anymore.

Fuck. It was Kenzie.

"I'd nail that ass so hard."

Without looking away from Kenzie he couldn't tell which of his sailors said it, but Brett slapped the table in the nonverbal command to shut it.

God, he couldn't argue with the statement, though. Kenzie looked sexy as all hell.

She wore a black dress that somehow managed to be sexy and modest as it hugged her every luscious curve. Her hair was down, looking extra shiny, and she was wearing makeup. There was no doubt in Brett's mind that the two were on a date.

Especially from the *you've got to be shitting me* look on her face as she followed Petersburg to a table full of men.

Several emotions slammed into him at once. Raw desire. Eagerness at seeing her again, and, most of all, guilt. Fuck, the guilt consumed the other two in a fiery rush.

Whatever rage she directed his way, he would take it.

Hell, he deserved it.

She hadn't seen him yet, that much was clear. He had to wonder if she'd make some kind of scene when she did. Though Kenzie hadn't given off the drama vibe the night they'd gone out.

Being a man who met conflict head on, he didn't even entertain the idea of trying to sneak off before she saw him. Instead he turned back in his seat, stretched his legs out under the table and stared straight ahead and kept his back to her.

Shit would hit the fan, or…fuck. They'd soon find out.

THIS GUY HAD to be fuckin' kidding. This was a first date. A bloody *first date* and he was going to squeeze them into a table full of random men she didn't know?

This was beginning to feel like the plot from some bad porno. Especially the way the first man had looked her over like she was the entrée at dinner. Next she'd learn the whole lot were construction workers or Navy men or something. Any minute now she expected to hear stripper music or some shite.

Kenzie's jaw ached from how tightly she clenched it and, for a moment, she debated turning on her completely impractical and painfully pretty heels and walking right back out the door.

Unfortunately, she'd chosen tonight to be the first time

in a while that she'd allowed her date to pick her up.

Though, hmm, she could always call Aleck. Then again *that* wouldn't turn out well. He'd lecture her for having the gall to try and date at nearly thirty, and threaten—again—to lock her up.

Folding her arms across her chest and lifting her chin to salvage pride, she approached the table of men with the same indifference she did when taking an order.

She slid a glance around the table of six men and bit back a groan. In fact, fuck it all, some of these men were regulars at the pub.

"Thanks for letting us crash your dinner, guys." Tad grinned, shaking hands with the men who stood up to greet them. "This is Kenzie, by the way," he said to the guys. "Kenzie, I used to serve with these guys in the Navy before I got out to take care of my son."

Oh shite, they literally were Navy men.

The introductions came next. Fast and furious, and she knew she'd never remember names—especially as they were last names only. She didn't miss the heated glances and big smiles that screamed *jackpot* as they checked her out.

"And then this here is Chief Craven. Probably the best guy you could pick to be your superior."

Kenzie was so caught up in the introductions that she hadn't paid much attention to the man sitting with his back to them.

He turned in his chair and the world around her spun.

Chapter Five

THE MAN WASN'T just any sailor, but him. Brett. Her date from seven months ago who'd gone AWOL. Her date was apparently a chief in the Navy. Even as a civilian, she knew that was a big deal. Just as rapidly as the shock at seeing him set in, it faded. She was good at landing on her feet.

Drawing in a quick breath, she did the same thing she'd done to the other sailors. She thrust out her hand and shook his. Keeping her expression blank, she murmured, "Nice to meet you, Mr. Craven."

Don't look him in the eyes.

Despite her vow not to, her gaze slid up from his broad chest, only to quickly make eye contact.

A mistake. There was a flash of surprise there—as if he were shocked she hadn't smashed him over the head with a glass, before his expression became a mask of politeness.

"Nice to meet you as well, Kenzie."

The bastard didn't even have the balls to call her out on her pretense that they didn't know each other. She'd expected a clever remark like "we've already met" or something. But then that would make him the type of man who dealt with his problems.

And that's what she was to him. A big old awkward problem who was about to plant herself firmly at his table.

"Have a seat. We've got plenty of room." Brett gestured to the two empty spots, not next to each other, of course.

This was turning out to be a piss-poor date.

At the last moment, two of the sailors jumped up from their seats to switch and give her and Tad seats next to one another. Though she wasn't sure if that was such a good thing, because right now he wasn't winning any points with her. Not to mention the switch put her directly across from Brett.

She hardly expected him to play footsies, but if he so much as tried anything he'd better be prepared to receive a foot in the balls.

Menus were passed their way as someone mentioned the rest of the guys had already ordered. In no time there were beers in front of them as conversation flowed.

Or rather, conversation flowed between the sailors, while she remained mostly silent. They made half-arsed attempts to include her, but it was clear the group hadn't seen each other in a while and were excited to catch up.

She snuck a glance over her menu at Brett, cursing her luck that while she was on her second date of the year, Brett—her first date of the year—was right across from her.

He cradled a water glass in his large hand, almost lounging in the wooden-backed chair. His position managed to be lazy and predatory at once.

She lifted her gaze higher, for a moment, and found those pale blue eyes watching her. His gaze was narrowed and heated.

Anger flashed through her and her lips tightened. He had no right to watch her this way—as if he were regretting standing her up. As if he were thinking about what she'd look like naked. He'd made a choice to walk away, so let the arse stew in his regret.

She tossed her hair over her shoulder and lifted her beer, arching a brow at him as she took a slow sip. Hopefully he could hear every blistering curse she was blasting him with in her head. Or at least imagine them.

His lips twitched into a grimace and he glanced away.

Aye, he knew.

The waitress arrived, and Kenzie put in an order for the fried pickles.

"Hey, you sure you want to get that?"

For a moment she wasn't sure she'd heard right, but sure enough, as she cast her date a disbelieving glance, she found him watching her with a critical frown.

"Excuse me?"

"The fried pickles." Tad leaned toward her and lowered his voice. "Look, you've been doing great with those ab workouts—you don't want to blow it for five minutes of greasy food that you'll regret."

Her face flushed with a stain of anger and embarrassment. This wanker had just called out her food choice at a table full of men. While they were on a first date. Clearly he wasn't gunning for a second one.

"I won't regret it. I'll work out another hour at the gym if I have to." She glanced around the table. "Or does anyone else feel I have some problem areas I should be working on?"

"Hell no," one guy chortled.

"You just keep doing whatever you're doing," the guy next to Brett muttered. "You're fucking hot."

In an instant Brett had smacked the guy lightly in the back of the head.

"Have some respect."

The sailor blushed. "Sorry, Chief."

"It's not me you need to apologize to."

"Sorry, Kenzie."

Most of them were drunk, she realized. The beer had kept coming, pint after pint. "It's all right. It's probably my fault for asking such a ridiculous question."

"Well, it followed an asinine comment," Brett murmured, casting a hard glance at Tad.

There was one thing they could agree on right now, but Tad didn't notice Brett's death glare because he was ordering another beer from the waitress.

Shite. She really ought to cut her losses and simply text one of the girls for a ride home, but there was food on the way and her beer to finish. No doubt about it, she *would* finish the beer because she'd sure as hell need it to get through this night.

An hour passed with more beer and food devoured. She'd picked at her own order, all too aware of Brett's heavy gaze on her most of the evening.

She'd felt the heat in it and was a bit shocked by the way her body responded. The heat that flowed through her veins and the quickening thud of her heart.

Why did it have to be him who affected her? After all this time of being numb to any kind of feminine reaction to a man. She had to get her knickers twisted over the one guy who'd made it painfully clear he didn't want to get involved with her.

Even if the way he watched her now clearly spoke otherwise. Had the others noticed the way Brett was watching her? Wouldn't they find it strange?

Then again, did it really matter? Once she left here tonight she had no intention of seeing any of them again. Though the gym might be difficult with Tad. Time to switch gyms. Oh hell, she hated working out, she may as well quit.

She cast Tad a sideways glance and sighed. Her date was now completely piss drunk. Fuck it all, she would have no choice but to call someone to give her a lift. There was no way she was climbing into a car with an intoxicated driver.

While the bill was settled, Kenzie sent a text to Hailey,

hoping her future sister-in-law was still awake.

Minutes ticked by and no reply came. Her heart sank.

"You ready to go?" Tad's words were slurred as he pushed back his chair and reached for her hand.

"I'll be taking her home."

Holy date hijacker, what? Kenzie swung a gaze toward Brett. What was he trying to pull?

Just barely, she managed to keep her tone polite. "That won't be necessary, thank you."

"Perhaps it's not, but I insist."

"Well insist all you want, I'll get my own bloody ride." Unable to control her temper any longer after such a shite evening, she shoved back her chair and stormed off to the bathroom to call Hailey.

BRETT WATCHED HER stride off away from the table, her hips swinging as she walked in those tiny heels. She was furious, and wonderfully sexy at it.

The pure male response slammed through him in a wash of desire that made his blood pound and his dick take notice. His awareness of her had been simmering all night and was damn near at boiling point.

It was more than her beauty. She had so much attitude and confidence. That confidence and somewhat lack of filter on her thoughts drew him to her even more.

He laid down some bills for the check, making sure he

paid for Kenzie's dinner as well, seeing that her date had screwed that up.

Glancing at the sailor who'd been deemed designated driver, Brett asked, "You'll be able to take Tad home too?"

"Sure, Chief, not a problem."

Confusion flashed across Tad's face. "Hey, wait a minute, that's *my* date. You're not really going to take her home are you?"

"If she can't find a ride from someone else, then yes." And he was hoping like hell she didn't, because the thought of her walking out that door and out of his life again made his chest tighten almost painfully.

He pushed back his chair, said good-bye to the group and made his way to the front of the restaurant.

Kenzie had disappeared into the bathroom, and he waited in the hall for her to reappear. When she finally did, she looked ticked off to the max. When she saw him her scowl deepened and her mouth compressed.

"You find a ride?" he asked quietly.

She lifted her chin and gave him a cool look. "I'll find one. Don't worry about it."

"It's in my nature to worry. Let me drive you home. You'll be safe."

"I don't doubt that, I simply don't much like you, Brett," she said bluntly. "I would rather ride on the back of an arthritic porcupine than drive home with you."

"Arthritic porcupine?" He blinked. "Slow and painful? Is

that what you were going for in that statement?"

"Sure, why not."

Her quirky sense of humor. Another check under reasons he was attracted to her.

"My truck's out front. How far are you from here?"

She hesitated, shaking her head. Finally: "Only a few miles."

"Let me drive you home." He stepped closer and lowered his voice. "It'll give me a chance to apologize."

Her eyes narrowed and she made a tiny sniff of disdain. "Little bit late, don't you think, *Chief?*"

There was no respect in the title, just derision.

"It's a lot late, but I'd really appreciate the opportunity regardless."

She pressed her lips together and he could see her internal argument. She gave a small, terse nod.

"Fine. I can't get ahold of my friends, would rather not call my brothers, and hate spending the money on a cab. Not that you can ever bloody find one around here."

He let out a breath of relief, not realizing he'd been holding it. He'd wanted this moment more than he'd imagined.

By habit, he placed a hand on the small of her back to guide her toward the door. The withering look she shot him had him starting to remove it, until a mocking voice stopped him.

"Well I'll be damned if my Highland hottie doesn't get around."

The tension in Kenzie's body was instant. He felt her spine stiffen against his fingertips, before she shocked him further by stepping backward, closer to him. As if seeking protection.

Brett turned to seek out the voice and found a man who looked to be in his early thirties coming down the hall from the bathroom.

"Arriving with one guy, leaving with another." The man grinned and took a step forward. "Actually, I've got to say, I'm surprised you didn't take the whole group of men home with you."

Oh the hell he did. Dropping his hand from Kenzie's back, Brett approached the other man.

"Is there a problem?" The blood in his veins began a hot, furious throbbing. "Just what the hell makes you think it's okay to talk to a lady that way?"

"Lady? Oh, Kenzie's no lady, are you, baby? Tell him about that time—"

Instinct had Brett's fist flying, but Kenzie grabbed his arm in record speed, barely stopping the punch. The man flinched and stepped back, looking completely shocked that someone would try and hit him.

"Stop," she pleaded, her words ragged. Pained. "He's not worth it, Brett. I promise."

Shit. She'd probably saved his ass. He blinked, realizing how close he'd come to giving this guy the beat-down he deserved. It might've gotten him dishonorably discharged from the Navy too.

One glance at Kenzie's white face and he realized his priorities needed to be her, not this piece of shit.

Taking a step toward the man, he said quietly, "You're lucky, douche bag. Damn lucky I'm not adding to those ugly scars on your face."

The man's expression turned to one of fury, as he reached up and touched a scarred cheek.

There was already a growing audience of people watching them with a fascination that was a bit unnerving. With Kenzie still clutching his arm, her expression furtive, Brett backed away.

"Let's get you home." He gave a terse nod and led her outside the restaurant.

When they were far enough away from the building he gave her a sideways glance.

Her face was still pale and her eyes had an alarming vacantness that was completely uncommon from what he knew of her.

"Are you all right?"

"Fine." The one word was devoid of emotion.

"The hell you are. Who was he?"

She gave a bitter laugh and a shake of her head. For a moment he figured she'd blow him off and give him some bullshit answer.

"Kenzie?"

"Charles Richland, otherwise known as the man who

roughed me up and attempted to rape me about a decade ago."

The truth knocked Brett sideways. He stumbled to a halt and caught her arm again, turning her to look at him.

"You're serious?"

"Aye. People generally don't encourage rape humor." She gave a twisted smile, and for a moment there was a flicker of emotion in her eyes.

"Jesus." He stopped and glanced back inside, almost wishing he'd punched the guy after all.

"If you don't believe me, it's fine. I'm quite used to it by now."

What the hell kind of statement was that? "Why would I not believe you?"

"Why would you? Either way, you don't really know me."

Crap, and that was completely his fault. "Maybe not, but you're not a complete stranger to me, and it's obvious that guy's a first-class D-bag."

"He is," she agreed.

"And I know enough about you to realize you wouldn't lie—especially about something this serious." He shook his head. "I'm sorry that happened to you, Kenzie. Both what happened five minutes ago, and back then."

She glanced up, seeming to search his face to see if he was being honest. She must've decided he was, because she relaxed a bit and nodded.

"Thank you. As I said, it was quite a while ago."

"Still, I hope he nearly rotted while serving time." He unlocked his truck and helped her in. "Though clearly if he's out now he didn't serve nearly enough."

She climbed past him into the cab of the pickup. "He didn't serve any."

His vision went red. "How in the hell does that happen? Did he get some bullshit community service sentence or something?"

"He was found not guilty. Technically, that upstanding citizen you had the pleasure of running into just now has a pristine record."

Brett's teeth snapped together as he shut Kenzie's door and moved around the truck to the passenger side.

Pristine record? Bullshit. If the man had gotten away with nearly raping a woman once, there was a good chance he'd succeeded after Kenzie.

Charles Richland. He'd have to remember that name and face.

Once he was settled behind the wheel, he hesitated before starting the ignition. Another thought began to creep in.

Kenzie had been almost skittish on their one date all those months ago. Seeming to fear being alone with him, and especially when he'd walked her out to the car. She'd almost gone into a panic.

Now he suspected the reason was because of an attack by that Richland guy.

"Are you waiting for something?"

He started the truck and shrugged. "Just lost in thought. Where are we going?"

She gave him directions to where he had a general idea of where to go. Driving down the highway, he murmured, "You seem to have bad luck with men."

Kenzie gave a choked gasp of disbelief. "Really? *You're* going to say that to me?"

"Maybe I shouldn't," he agreed. "It just started to sink in."

"Aye, well include yourself among that bloody list of men then."

He didn't even deflect that blow, because he deserved it. "I do, and I'm sorry."

He felt her gaze on him. Hard. Questioning.

"I know it's been over a half a year since that night, but are you going to tell me why, Brett? I thought we had a pretty good connection. I had fun. Silly me, but I thought you enjoyed yourself too—"

"I did enjoy myself."

"You did," she repeated hesitantly. "Then why did you drop me on my arse? When you were so persistent in getting me to go out with you in the first place? Was it because I didn't sleep with you that night?"

How did he answer that? He'd been raised in a family where he was taught the truth was the easiest answer. Not always the most pleasant, but often the easiest. When you were honest, you didn't have to keep track of the lies you told.

"Partly, yes." He glanced over in time to see hurt flash across her face.

"Well, I'll give you credit for having the balls to admit it," she muttered, looking away.

"It's not in my nature to lie. I did want to sleep with you, Kenzie. When I came there that night, the only thoughts in my head were of finding you and ultimately getting you into my bed."

She made a soft grunt of disgust and kept her gaze out the window.

"But then there was dinner and we connected on this deeper level. Then there was the tiny kiss that turned out to be so fucking hot. And you were just too sweet. Too vulnerable." His voice roughened as he made the acknowledgment to himself and to her.

He'd sensed that about her before knowing why. Though he knew better than to call her out on it.

"Turn here, and it'll be the last house on the right," she instructed tersely. "And those aren't words people usually associate with me. I'm not vulnerable."

The hell she wasn't. Clearly she hated the idea of being vulnerable, but she was. Maybe she hid it well, but her guard had come down that night, and then a few minutes ago inside the restaurant when Charles had taunted her.

He parked outside her house and sighed. "Regardless,

Kenzie, I liked you a little too much. I couldn't get involved with you and hurt you that way, because I don't do permanent."

She tilted her head, giving him a blistering look. "And you made the bloody assumption that I was looking for a husband and passed me by because of it?"

Maybe? Shit. He wasn't even sure. When she climbed out of the car, he followed after her.

"I don't know what I assumed, I only knew that you deserved more than a one-night stand."

She turned around, nearly causing him to ram into her. "Maybe a one-night stand was what I was searching for."

Once he acclimated to the temptation of her being so close, he focused on her words. They were almost convincing, but he was skilled enough at reading people to see past her bluff. But he'd play along if that's what she wanted.

"Was it?"

Her cockiness vanished and she bit her lip. "No, but I'm not looking for anything serious yet, either. I want something in between."

"And that's why you went out with this clown tonight?"

Her chin came up. "Tad is a nice guy. He simply made a few bad choices tonight."

"You think? I sure as shit wouldn't tell you what to eat. Or bring you on what equates to a group date. Or—"

"You *sure as shit* have no place to judge." Her eyes flashed a warning.

Tad had been kind of an asshole while serving in the Navy, and tonight Brett had realized he had only gotten worse. Yet here she was defending him.

Irritation slid through his veins and he took a step forward, bringing them even closer together.

"Maybe not, but I know you deserve better. I didn't walk away so some other asshole could scoop you up."

"Scoop me up? FYI, I'm not an ice cream cone. Step one in the asshole rehabilitation process is admitting you're one—so kudos to you." Her green eyes were sparkling with anger now, and another emotion he knew she wouldn't want him to see.

There was a hint of awareness. Of heat that had nothing to do with anger. She was still attracted to him and probably hated herself for it.

He was out of line; there was no doubt about it. Still, he placed his hands on the door on either side of her body, lightly trapping her. He waited for the slightest hint of fear or unease in her eyes. If he saw it, he'd step back. There was none, only the slight hitch of her breathing and the flare of anticipation in her gaze.

"You're right. I'm a complete asshole, because all I can think about right now is this."

He dipped his head, claiming her mouth in a kiss that he had no right to take. It was the only place their bodies touched, their lips fused together as he braced himself against the door.

Needing more than that first, almost innocent kiss they'd shared, he teased the seam of her lips apart and slid his tongue inside to discover the taste of her.

She was as sweet as he'd imagined, and not for the first time he kicked himself for walking away. He deepened the kiss, all the while keeping in mind that he had to give her space to say no. To push him off her.

But right now she was making no move to do either. Instead she was kissing him back, almost tentatively. Her tongue meeting his in small, hesitant strokes.

Need coursed through his body, heavy and demanding, and he couldn't help but release a small groan against her mouth.

It took a moment for him to register her hands on his shoulders, gently pushing him away.

"Enough," she said raggedly.

Struggling to focus, he stared down at her. Her lips pink and moist, her gaze lowered beneath her lashes.

"Kenzie?"

"My roommate's not here. I don't have to work tonight. I could invite you inside and we'd have the house to ourselves."

He moved a hand to cup her face, unable to resist touching the softness of her lips. Yet his gut clenched, because he knew where she was heading with this.

"You could, but you won't."

"I won't. Because nothing's changed in seven months.

I'm still not *that* girl. Not the kind who sleeps with a guy right away."

"And what if I said I'd wait until you were ready?"

She gave a disbelieving laugh. "You didn't wait the first time before you ran out to find someone else. You're hardly going to wait a second." She fished her keys from her purse.

He latched on to one thing she'd said. "Hold on a moment. What makes you think I found someone else?"

She shrugged, shoving the key into the lock. "I saw you guys at Safeway. Does it matter?"

What the hell? Safeway. He racked his memory, but was coming up empty.

After pushing the door open, she hesitated.

"At one point there was a real window of opportunity for something between us. But…it's closed now." Her gaze lifted to his once more, and her expression was resolute, if not a little sad. "Thanks for the ride."

The door closed in his face a moment later. Brett stood there staring at the dark wood, a frown tugging at his mouth.

Who the hell was the woman she'd seen him with at Safeway?

Chapter Six

"HEY, HOW WAS your date the other night?"

Kenzie set the drink tray down at the counter and grimaced at Delonna's question.

"Pretty bloody awful, actually."

"You've got to be shitting me." Delonna grabbed the empty glasses off it and pulled it behind the bar. "How does it get more awful than your last one?"

"Oh you know, ending up at a table full of Navy men, one being your date from seven months ago who disappeared off the face of the earth."

"Wait, that Brett guy was there?"

"Aye." Kenzie glanced around the pub, glad to see the dinner rush was mediocre at best. Even if it meant fewer tips, she needed a long break tonight to get some homework done for her online class.

"Well crap. That's awkward."

"Mmm. To say the least."

"I'm not sure I understand why you ended up with a bunch of Navy guys in the first place. Wasn't this a first date with the personal trainer?"

"I'm not sure I understand either, and yes, it was a first date. The restaurant Tad picked was surprisingly crowded and we would've waited at least a half hour for a table. He saw some friends who invited us over, and, bam, horribly uncomfortable moment with Brett ensues."

Delonna scowled. "Did you give him shit for being an asshole? Dump your beer on him or anything?"

"No. I simply got through the evening." She glanced away, hoping her friend wouldn't see the flush of embarrassment in her face.

No need to mention she'd climbed into his truck and then kissed him good night. It was one bad call after another.

And yet that kiss was hard to regret. It had been just as titillating as the first one. Actually quite a bit more. Especially when he'd pressed his tongue into her mouth—it was almost juvenile the pleasure she'd taken in it. She was nearing thirty and how a French kiss could be so seductive and stay in her mind for days now was mind-boggling.

Or maybe it wasn't the kiss, but the man behind it. She suspected that had more to do with it. She'd been right to send him on his way, though. Everything she'd told him had been the truth. If he'd been hoping to get laid, then he would've been sorely disappointed.

As much as she sometimes wished she worked that way, her mind and heart wouldn't allow her to simply jump into bed the minute her hormones begged for it.

"Did he apologize?"

Kenzie glanced up to see Delonna pulling her blonde hair back into a ponytail.

"Brett?"

"Well, Brett and Tad both owed you one it sounds like."

"Tad, somewhat. Brett, aye. He did."

"Did he explain why he disappeared on you?"

"Said something about him not doing serious."

"And he figured you were looking for a ring?" Delonna rolled her eyes. "Typical guy."

"Who's looking for a ring?" Aleck wandered out from the room at the back of the pub. His gaze skimmed the dining room before sliding back to Delonna and Kenzie. "Not one of you, I hope."

Delonna gave a low laugh. "Bitch, please, I'm not getting married until I'm at least twenty-six."

Kenzie smirked. At any other job, someone might've gotten fired, if not written up, for calling their boss a bitch, but for these two it was everyday banter.

"Twenty-six?" Aleck arched a brow. "That'd be in, what, ten years or so?"

"Right, because I just had my sweet sixteen last week." Delonna swatted a towel at his arse as he walked by.

He laughed and deftly avoided the stinging slap. "Watch it, or I'll have to properly discipline you."

"Oh, you're not offering to turn me over your knee are you, boss boy?" She batted her lashes. "Because, I gotta say,

I'm kind of into that sort of thing."

Kenzie glanced over at her brother just in time to see shock and a tiny bit of interest flicker in his eyes as he stared at Delonna, but then it was gone and he gave a small shake of his head.

"You are the epitome of trouble, Delonna."

"So I've been told."

When Aleck disappeared out onto the dining floor again, Kenzie turned to her friend.

"I swear you have some sick reverse sexual harassment thing going on here with him."

"He likes it."

"I have no doubt, actually. It's probably a good thing you're involved with someone or he'd be tempted to go after you."

Delonna snorted and glanced off to where Aleck had disappeared. "He's so busy chasing skirts he doesn't even notice me."

Kenzie gave a small grunt in reply. Delonna was safe from her brother for the time being. Not only was she a bit young for him, but he also stayed away from taken women and Delonna had been in a relationship for the past year.

"Speaking of being involved with someone." Delonna cleared her throat. "Did James and I keep you awake last night? We were a little loud."

Oh yes, Kenzie had heard Delonna and her boyfriend being a bit noisy in bed on more than one occasion. But then that was likely the joy of having a roommate.

"Not last night. I was out like a light from exhaustion."

"Okay, good. I always get worried…"

"No need to apologize, Delonna. You're having fun and I have nothing against that."

Delonna grinned. "Oh, James is most definitely fun. He does this thing with his beard—"

"And you can stop at fun!" Kenzie ran the words together, covering her ears with her hands. "I can't unsee that shite in my head now, damn you."

Delonna's laughter followed her as Kenzie made her way back into the dining area. Her footsteps faltered at the sight of the vase of gorgeous flowers on an empty table and the card next to it.

Flowers that hadn't been there a few minutes ago.

Frowning, Kenzie moved to pick them up and spotted her name on the card.

Her gaze flew to the table across the way where an older couple sat eating.

"You didn't happen to see who dropped this off, did you?"

The pair shrugged.

"I think I saw a young man come in a moment ago," the woman replied, "but we were enjoying our fish and chips and didn't pay much attention. Those are lovely flowers, though, dear."

Aye, they were.

"Thank you," Kenzie murmured absently and carried the card and flowers to the back room.

She sat down at Aleck's desk and admired the mix of pink daisies and red roses. Before she opened the card, she dipped her head to breathe in the lovely scent. Maybe it was a way to stall before opening the card. They had to be from Tad, who hadn't stopped calling or leaving messages.

In the messages he was most apologetic and embarrassed about his behavior on Friday night. She'd almost felt sorry for him, until in one of the last messages he'd asked—with a slightly whiny tone—if Brett had made a move on her.

None of your fuckin' business, Tad.

Her lips twitched as she pried open the envelope and pulled out a card. Before she could read it, several pictures fell out and hit the desk. Frowning, she picked them up and noticed one seemed quite dated. There was a little boy of maybe seven and a girl several years younger.

The girl was crying over a scoop of ice cream that had fallen off her cone, and the boy was pointing and laughing.

Interesting. Her lips quirked as she flipped to the next one. A picture of the same kids, a few years older at Disney World, riding the Dumbo ride together.

The boy was starting to look somewhat familiar. She glanced at a couple more before arriving at the last one. She drew in a ragged breath as she stared at the grown man and woman, standing on Deception Pass Bridge, with the man's arm around her shoulders.

Setting the pictures down, she finally read the card that clearly wasn't from Tad.

The woman you saw me with at Safeway was my sister. She was out visiting from Louisiana.

Look, I know I screwed up. I never even gave us a chance based on my asinine assumption that you were looking for something serious.

I can't get you out of my head, and I want you like I've never wanted another woman. To the point where there have been no other women.

Please, Kenzie, give me another chance. Those two kisses were just the beginning. You know we'd be explosive.

~Brett

She stared at the phone number below his name, knowing he'd left the ball in her court. Her pulse quickened and her stomach was doing little flips, but even still she couldn't trust it completely.

And what did he mean by no other women? She snorted and tossed down the card on top of the pictures. Surely he didn't expect her to believe that he hadn't slept with anyone recently? He was a sexy man in his prime, a chief in the Navy. It was pretty certain that women likely threw themselves at his feet.

What kind of shite line was that?

"Everything all right back here?"

Seeing her brother enter the back room, Kenzie scrambled to her feet and collected the pictures and card.

"Fine. Everything's just fine."

"Good." Aleck nodded, his expression unreadable. "Who are the flowers from?"

"Flowers? Oh right, these flowers. They're from Sarah. She knew I wasn't feeling well the other day and sent them. Emily helped pick them out." Lie. Crap but she was lying to her own brother. What was wrong with her?

"Oh aye? That's right decent of her."

His words went along with it, but she knew her brother well enough to realize he was suspicious. If it had been another situation, anyone else, she might have admitted the truth. But she saw no point in dragging Brett into her brother's life, especially seeing as they'd gotten off to a bad start.

Besides, even though the note and flowers were a nice gesture, it still seemed like a bad idea to try and get involved with Brett. Maybe she wasn't looking for a ring right now, but as he'd guessed, she wasn't exactly looking for a one-night stand either.

"I should get back up front. Thought I'd just rest my feet for a bit." She struggled to gather the flowers, card and pictures in her hands and scooted past him.

Out in the pub again, she moved behind the counter to stuff the pictures and card into her purse. Only the card wasn't in her hand.

Shite.

Alarmed, she spun on her heels to race back to the office and grab the card, which must've fallen out of her grasp.

Aleck pushed open the door before she could get anywhere near it. He held the card up and gave her a narrowed look.

"How about you share who this bastart is?"

Her teeth snapped together and she seethed out a breath, before shaking her head. "You read it? You had no bloody right, Aleck. That's my business."

"Where you're concerned, it is my business. You lied to me and said this was from Sarah."

"So? I'm a grown woman," she snapped, grabbing the card from him, "but even if I was fourteen, you should respect my privacy."

"I do it out of concern, and because I care, Kenzie."

"Well sometimes you care a little too much."

"Wait, you read her card?" Delonna came up beside them and shook her head. "Not cool."

"This doesn't bloody well concern you, Delonna. Go do your fookin' job."

"Jeez. Someone forgot to take their Midol." Delonna's words were tight and there was a hint of shock and hurt in her eyes.

This was the first time Kenzie could remember her brother having yelled at the younger woman.

When Delonna disappeared back behind the counter, Kenzie turned to glare at her brother again.

"Well wasn't that just lovely of you. Let's take this outside, shall we, Brother?"

Without waiting for him to finish, she turned and marched out of the pub to the nearly empty parking lot.

Aleck followed her, as she knew he would.

"Are you serious about him?"

She knew from the tension in his voice he was trying to sound calm.

Appreciating the effort, she grimaced. "There's nothing to be serious over. We had one date."

"Clearly he's hoping for—"

"Aye, I know what he's hoping for."

Aleck's gaze darkened. "Who is he?"

She would not admit he was the guy from the bar who Aleck had confronted all those months ago.

"It doesn't matter," she said softly. "Aleck, you need to let me live my life."

"Have I not done that? You've moved out on your own."

"That's a big step, aye, but it's more than that. You need to trust that I can make big-girl decisions regarding the men in my life, and as much as it may bug the lot of you, some day there will be a man who's just as important to me as the McLaughlin brothers."

Aleck's scowl deepened. "That may be so, but I don't much care for this wanker."

"You don't know him."

"Are you serious about him?"

"You already asked me that." She sighed. "I'll not be seeing him anymore. It didn't work between us."

"Did he hurt you?"

Yes, but she'd never admit that. "It simply didn't work, Aleck. Please. I'll not ask again. Let me handle my love life without interference from my big brother."

Aleck stared at her, his gaze searching hers. Finally he nodded, thrusting a hand through his hair.

"I know you're right. It's just hard not to be protective of my little sister. Especially after Charles, who we all thought was a nice guy." He gave a cold laugh. "I want to vet every man who comes into your life, and I'm not alone. Ian and Colin feel the same."

"I know you all do, and if it wasn't so maddening, it'd be sweet."

"I'm sorry, Kenzie. I'll let you be." Aleck pulled her into a hug. "But if he hurts you, I'll bloody well hurt *him*."

In his arms she frowned. "I just told you I have no intention—"

"Your eyes tell me something else. You're interested in him, whether you realize it or not."

Well if that wasn't complete shite.

She walked back into the pub a few minutes later, her mood heavier and her irritation at an elevated level.

"What should we do with these flowers?" Delonna asked, lifting the bouquet from the counter.

It was on the tip of Kenzie's tongue to tell her to toss them. But they were beautiful, and he'd likely spent too much money on them.

"Here, I'll take them." She took the flowers from Delonna and went to give them to the elderly couple in the restaurant.

~

NOTHING. THAT WAS the response he'd gotten from Kenzie after he'd sent flowers and a carefully planned-out card filled with old pictures.

Sitting in his recliner after a tiring day at work, Brett sighed and flipped the channel from the baseball game to the news.

One week and there'd been nothing but silence. Which was pretty much exactly what he'd done to her after their first and only date. Except instead of a week, it had been over seven months. And there really was no way to get back onto someone's radar with a fuckup that massive.

He should just give up on the idea of her now. There were plenty of women out there who'd made their interest in him known, but, hell, they may as well have been cardboard cutouts. There was no attraction. No chemistry. It had become a major problem. No woman had stimulated him on a mental and physical level the way Kenzie had.

Maybe if they hadn't had that second kiss, that hot-as-hell second kiss on her doorstep, she might've been able to convince him she wasn't interested.

But the way she kissed him back said otherwise. She

didn't want serious, but she didn't want a one-night stand. Since his last girlfriend, he didn't stick around with a woman for more than a month. It was a self-imposed rule he stayed pretty rigid to. Self-preservation and all.

The news went to a commercial and he scrubbed a hand down his jaw, sighing with frustration. No woman should take up this much of his thoughts. She'd successfully occupied his mind for over a year now. That was insane for a woman he wasn't even sleeping with.

The words of the commercial registered and he turned his focus to the screen. Frowning, he watched the images flash across it. Bagpipes, women and children dancing, some kind of games involving a long pole, and then lots of men in kilts. The Highland Games. This was a local commercial for the upcoming Highland Games.

He sat up straighter. Kenzie was Scottish. Her family ran a Scottish pub. It was a long shot, but maybe there was a chance she went to these sorts of things.

It was this weekend. Two days from now. Chances were there was a group of sailors who'd be heading over there. Maybe he could tag along on the ruse of needing to get some culture. Or some kind of bullshit.

Right now, he just wanted another chance to see her. If it meant showing up at some testosterone-laden event, then he'd damn well do it.

Yeah, tomorrow morning, he'd ask around the base and see who was up for it.

Chapter Seven

THIS WAS ABSOLUTELY nothing like what he'd expected. Brett glanced around the Highland Games and frowned slightly. It had almost a street fair atmosphere. Food booths, shopping booths, informational booths and various stages and areas where events were happening.

"They have a whisky-tasting thing, Chief, and I think we should hit that up."

Brett glanced over at Simmons. "It's barely past noon."

The sailor grinned. "Exactly. I already had my coffee. You coming?"

"Later. I'm going to wander for a bit. I'll meet you guys over there."

"All right. Later, Chief." Simmons took off with a group of about five other sailors who were also under Brett's command.

He bit back a sigh. Those guys drank a little too much maybe, but then, it was somewhat their age and lifestyle too. A lot of these young, unmarried sailors simply wanted to drink and get laid when they weren't working. Lather, rinse, repeat.

Hell, he'd gone through a similar phase, but he was done with that shit now. Everything in moderation. Especially the drinking, and he rarely did that around his men anyway.

Brett stood where he was, glancing around the grounds and debating where to go first. The sound of bagpipes resonated in the warm afternoon. He could follow them. Maybe there was some kind of parade or something. He glanced down at the schedule he'd picked up and scanned it.

The games portion of the event seemed to involve mostly men. Maybe he should check out the Highland dancing stage. There were various activities going on all day there.

He wandered over to the area, his gaze roaming the crowd for any sight of her. Finally he arrived at the stage where some of the dancing seemed to be taking place. Disappointment sank in as he watched the group of children performing onstage.

Children. Not the beautiful, grown Scottish woman he was hoping for. Still, he was so impressed by the little kids and their athletic dance to the bagpipes, that he sat down in one of the chairs to watch. Not to mention he was beginning to realize finding Kenzie here was a long shot.

The dance wrapped up and the children rushed offstage. His gaze naturally followed them, his lips twisting in amusement at their level of excitement.

There she was. His breath caught as he spotted her. Kenzie stood off to the side of the stage, embracing one of the little girls and clearly offering up praise.

He realized immediately why he hadn't recognized her right away. Her most recognizable feature, her hair, was twisted in a bun on top of her head. Her makeup was dark, and she wore some kind of traditional Scottish dance outfit: a long tartan skirt, and white blouse with a black vest over it, and some weird high-rise socks.

The outfit was about as non-sexy as you could get, and yet the only thought in his mind was how damn beautiful she was.

He watched from his seat near the back as the children transitioned offstage and a smaller adult group of female dancers replaced them. Just like the rest of the women, Kenzie was all smiles as the performance began.

She exchanged a glance with another dancer and threw back her head and laughed in delight. Clearly she loved this and dancing was her element. She was damn good at it.

Her gaze turned to the crowd, her smile wide. It faltered the moment she spotted him. So did her steps, but she quickly recovered. Her gaze swept away from him and her smile—more strained now—widened.

Brett stayed and watched the rest of the show, and it wasn't one hundred percent because of Kenzie.

He watched in surprise and growing fascination at how athletic the dance was. Lots of kicking and jumping, and pretty much staying on their toes. Clearly this was at least part of how she kept in such good shape.

When the dance came to an end, the dancers exited the stage and clustered around chatting. Not Kenzie, though. She made a beeline straight for him.

"I don't suppose your being here is a coincidence?" She propped a hand on her hip and gave him a pointed look.

"I've got a thing for Scottish chicks?"

Her gaze narrowed, but he swore he saw her mouth twitch.

"One in particular," he added quietly. "That was some pretty impressive dancing there."

"Thank you."

Was the flush in her cheeks from his compliment, or from the dancing? Either way, he hadn't noticed it a moment ago.

"I'm sorry you didn't receive my flowers."

"I did." She must've realized her mistake in the admission a moment too late. Guilt flashed briefly in her eyes. "They were lovely. Thank you."

"Sure they didn't end up in the garbage?"

"Of course not. I gave them to a cute older couple having supper in the pub."

Well, at least that wasn't quite as bad as the garbage. Though the garbage had probably been the final resting place for his pictures and the card.

"Why are you trying so hard, Brett?"

"Because I can't stop thinking about you."

She stared at him a moment before doing an aggravating

eye roll.

"And how many women have you used that on? Because it sounds like one of the most cliché lines in the book."

"Maybe I have used it before," he admitted. "But I'm pretty sure you're the only one I've actually meant it about."

"I'm not quite sure if that's endearing or insulting. It does, however, sound like another line." Her mouth curved into a half smile, before she glanced behind her at someone. The child she'd been embracing earlier.

"Who's she?"

"My niece." Her tone warmed. "She only took up the dancing less than a year ago."

He remembered the girl from the stage. She was a cute little thing.

"She did great."

"Aye, she did." Pride clearly resonated in Kenzie's tone. Finally she turned to face him. "What will it take you to leave me be?"

"Do you really want me to?"

She opened her mouth, but then closed it again. Then she drew her bottom lip between her teeth and nibbled. God, but he wanted to be the one nibbling on the pink flesh.

"I didn't call you," she muttered, almost churlishly.

"Maybe you lost the card with my number on it."

She arched a brow. "Maybe I threw it away on purpose."

Actually, that was probably exactly what she'd done.

"Have a drink with me," he commanded softly. "Or is

there somewhere else you need to be? Do you have to watch your niece?"

"No. She's going to watch her dad compete in several events in the games. Her mother's taking her."

He glanced beyond her to see the girl walking beside someone who must've been the mother. Both shared olive coloring and a somewhat exotic look about them.

"I have nowhere else to be, but give me a moment." She disappeared briefly to talk to the woman.

The woman nodded, glanced his way curiously, and then walked off with the little girl.

"So that was a yes to the drink?" he queried when she returned.

"Do you drink whisky?" She answered his question with one of her own.

Not since he'd overindulged twelve years ago with a group of sailors and had been sicker than a dog.

"I have." Ambiguity was always good.

"Let's go do a tasting, if you think you can handle it."

Damn, but had she just thrown down a challenge or what?

"Sugar, I'm at least half a foot taller and probably close to a hundred pounds more. I think I can handle it."

"Right then." She arched a brow and strode past him. "Shall we?"

∽

KENZIE LED BRETT to the cordoned-off area that was designated for the twenty-one and older crowd. With him walking behind her, she was fairly certain he had a great view of her arse, but what did it matter? There wasn't much to see being that it was hidden beneath her heavy tartan skirt.

"Hello, Kenzie!"

As they moved into the tasting area, people started waving and greeting her. She knew these people well and saw them frequently at the different Highland Games locations.

"Good afternoon, Patrick. I've brought a friend in for a lesson on whisky."

"All right." The older man glanced at Brett and grinned. "Have a seat, and I'll get you both started. Though Kenzie could probably run it herself, seeing as she has before."

"Oh, you flatter me." She winked at Patrick and took a seat at the table.

As the older man began preparing for their sampling, Brett's mouth suddenly thinned as he looked over her shoulder. A moment later she heard the roars and taunting of men behind her.

She turned and saw a group of young men approaching. Several of them familiar from their group dinner the other night.

"Hey, Chief, isn't that Tad's girl?" one called out, clearly a little buzzed already.

"My name is Kenzie, since you seem to be struggling to recall, and I'm nobody's girl." She gave them a saccharine yet bitchy smile.

Her response only encouraged them and they started hollering and clapping.

"She told you, Wilks."

"Your whisky." Patrick returned with two shot glasses and three bottles of whisky. "Shall I begin?"

Kenzie leaned over and gave him her most innocent, imploring smile, then asked quietly, "Actually, Patrick, I quite like the idea of running this one myself. Would you mind terribly? I'll leave you my credit card to cover my arse in case."

Patrick blushed and looked around. "Oh, well, I don't see the harm in it. You've run this more than once. I'll be nearby if you need me."

Once he disappeared, she turned back to face Brett.

"All right. Let's get started."

"Where did the other dude go? Patrick?" Brett looked slightly alarmed.

"He put you in my hands. You're not worried, are you?"

"I'd be all right in her hands," one of the sailors yelled, causing the rest to guffaw.

Little boys. They were like little fuckin' boys.

"That's enough," Brett called out tersely, and the group immediately stood straighter and quieted.

They truly did respect him and his authority, even when not at work.

"All right. I have three bottles of whisky here. One is

considered average, the other high-end, and the last more of a bargain one. Which shall we try first?"

"Bargain."

Ah, now that surprised her. She fancied him for the high-end type of guy. The group of sailors seemed to grow bored and disappeared back to their own drinks.

She filled Brett's glass with two fingers of whisky and then her own.

Brett reached for it immediately.

"Now I want you to—"

Before she could finish he'd tossed it back, swallowing the shot in one single gulp.

"Amateur." She couldn't help but laugh.

"Excuse me?" His eyes were watering and he wiped his mouth with the back of his hand.

"You're not to shoot the drink. We sip it. I want you to savor it and enjoy the complexity of the drink."

"Complexity? It tastes like whisky. Isn't that about all there is to it?"

She shook her head and refilled his shot. "Let's try this again. Sip it. Tell me what you notice."

They took a sip together, and he closed his eyes for a moment, seeming to be considering it.

"This one burns." He opened his eyes and shrugged. "Honestly, it kind of tastes like ass."

"So lovely to hear that you're familiar with the taste of ass," she teased dryly and finished the rest of her shot.

Brett didn't laugh, but remained silent. In his gaze she only saw a smoldering heat that made her realize maybe she shouldn't have said something so completely suggestive.

"Finish that and we'll try the mid-grade whisky."

He tossed back the shot and winced. "Yeah, it's pretty gross. Sorry."

"Glenfiddich is actually quite popular." She filled up his glass with the next bottle. "What is your usual drink of preference?"

"Brandy."

"Ah. Very classic."

"Is it?" He lifted the glass and sniffed. "This one smells different. Smoky."

"Aye. Try it. Let me know what you think."

She watched him lift the glass to his mouth and take a small drink. He pursed his lips and nodded.

"That's pretty damn good. Tastes smoky."

"That's what Bowmore is legendary for. They're produced in the second-oldest distillery in Scotland." She drank hers and then reached for the third bottle. "And here is our high-end Tomatin whisky."

Almost a pro at this now, Brett took a small sip and nodded. "It's smooth."

"Aye." She drank it back easily. "It's my favorite. Well, one of them."

He tossed back the rest of the shot and arched a brow. "You have expensive tastes, Ms. McLaughlin."

"Mmm. Only in my whisky." She refilled her glass with another shot.

"That's it?" He arched a brow. "We're done?"

"You've had four shots, I think that's enough." She gave him a sweet smile and then downed hers.

His brows drew together as if she'd insulted him. "Is there more whisky to sample?"

"Oh, aye, there's plenty."

He pushed his glass toward her. "Well let's keep going."

"I wouldn't want you to get drunk." She arched a brow.

"If you're not drunk, sugar, then I'm nowhere near it."

Really? She wasn't going to point out how his eyes were brighter than they had been a few minutes ago.

"Oh right. Because you're so much taller and heavier," she murmured sweetly and stood to retrieve a couple more bottles.

Ten minutes and three shots later, she could feel the buzz coming on and she leaned back in her chair and stared at Brett.

He nursed his glass in his hand, a slightly dopey smile on his face. "You're gorgeous."

"Thank you."

"No really. You're gorgeous." He leaned forward, propping an elbow on the table. "And you're smart—oops." His elbow wobbled and he fell forward slightly.

"And I think we've had enough of this." She stood, grabbed the bottles and returned them easily.

Her stomach was warm and she had a mild buzz, meaning she'd either be here until evening before she drove, or she'd be catching a ride home.

But Brett, now he was pretty much—

"I can't believe it. Is the chief drunk?"

She turned at the voice, and gave the approaching sailors a wry smile.

"Aye, he might be a bit. I think he overestimated his tolerance for whisky. Will one of you be able to drive him home?"

"Drive me home?" Brett stumbled to his feet. "I'm fine."

"Are you?"

"No, actually, I'm not." He frowned and dismay slowly spread across his face. "Dammit, you got me drunk."

"I believe you got yourself drunk, Chief," she said sweetly. "Perhaps you'd do well to know your limits next time."

"How are you still sober?" He was slurring his *s*'s right now. "I would be so damn pissed right now if you weren't so gorgeous." He stumbled forward. "Can I at least get a kiss?"

His sailors were having a field day with this. She could see it in her peripheral. The nudging of each other and little effort to restrain their laughter.

"No, you may not get a kiss." She patted him on the shoulder and winked. "What you may want to get are a few painkillers before bed. Drink lots of water, and perhaps eat some bread."

"Bread. That doesn't sound—oh my *God*." He spun to

the group of sailors. "Which one of y'all is driving me home? Can we go to Taco Heaven?"

Unable to hide her mirth now, she joined in with the laughing sailors. A few stepped forward to help escort him out of the cordoned-off whisky area.

"Make sure he gets home safely?" she asked the sailor who looked most trustworthy. Really, it was a shot in the dark at this rate.

"Yes, ma'am." He grinned. "We've been trying to get Chief drunk for years. You accomplished what we've never managed to do."

Guilt stabbed briefly through her, but she kept her smile up.

"He's probably not drunk," she lied, "but it's best you drive him just in case."

"He's tossed on his ass. I'm pretty sure he'll puke to-night."

"I hope not," she murmured, worrying her lip with her teeth. God, what if he actually got sick in their car? Yikes.

Brett was half led, half carried past her.

"You're gorgeous, Kenzie," he called out again.

And then he broke into that *don't you forget about me* song as he was led out of the fairgrounds.

"What the hell kind of nonsense was that?"

She turned to find her brother Colin standing behind her, scowling. How long had he been there?

"What nonsense?" she asked innocently.

"You got that man pissed drunk. Why?"

She blushed. Damn good question. "He overestimated his tolerance level."

"You don't mess around with a man like that, Kenz. He'll not take it well in the morning. Do you know him?"

"Aye, she does." Aleck appeared next, a dark expression on his face as he glanced after the retreating sailors. "So it was him? He brought the card. I should've known."

"Aleck…"

"You made your bed, you can lie in it." He shook his head. "That was dirty. You knew he'd try to keep up with a woman, and your tolerance is higher than most men's with whisky. It near runs in your veins."

Aye, of course she knew. That's why she'd brought Brett over here.

The guilt inside her spread, not fading even after her brothers left her again and the sailors had long since disappeared.

Shite.

Aleck was right. Brett was going to be a mess come morning, and embarrassed as hell.

She'd fucked up, and good.

Chapter Eight

OH FUCK. HIS head hurt like someone was taking a baseball bat to it.

Lying in bed, Brett contemplated getting up to find some kind of painkiller. But that would mean getting up. He lay there for a while, memories of yesterday seeping into his consciousness and bringing horror and humiliation.

Holy shit. He'd gotten drunk. In front of Kenzie. In front of his sailors. So drunk that they'd had to nearly carry him out of the fairgrounds.

More memories came, this time of him shoveling nachos and burritos down his throat. Taco Heaven. He hadn't been there since he was a teenager and his cousin had gotten him high. Had he…had he actually *begged* his sailors to take him there?

Groaning, Brett pulled the pillow over his head to help block out the morning light. Block out the memories. The pounding in his head didn't stop, though. It took a few seconds to realize that the pounding was coming from his front door.

Probably one of his men coming to check on his ass.

Swinging his legs out of bed, he stumbled to the front door—ready to tell whomever it was to get lost. He unlocked the door and bolt and then swung it open. With the sunlight glaring behind the person, it took a minute to figure out who it was, but soon a very definite female silhouette took form.

"Can I come in?"

Kenzie. For once, he had absolutely no desire to see her.

"No."

He tried to shut the door and she grabbed it, pushing it back open. She was stronger than she looked, he mused, or he was too weak and hungover.

"What are you doing here?" It was a near-snarl.

"You told me not to forget about you, remember?" She gave him a cheerful smile and closed the door behind them.

"What the hell are you talking about?"

"Yesterday…" Her words trailed off and her gaze slid over him, lingering on his bare chest. She swallowed hard.

Never one to be self-conscious, he wasn't about to start now. Besides, he had on boxers and that was practically overdressed for the hell his body was going through.

"It doesn't…never mind." She shook her head and blinked, adjusting the paper bag in her hand. "Have you taken anything for your head?"

"No."

"Go lie your arse back down. I'll bring you something." And she disappeared into his house as if she'd been there a hundred times.

How the hell did she even figure out where he lived in the first place?

He wanted to argue, but his damn head pounded with every breath he drew in. This was why he didn't drink whisky. He should've known better. Should've read more into that twinkle in Kenzie's eye when she'd made the offer to go sample some.

He crawled back into bed, beyond the point of worrying about pride, and pulled the blanket over his head. Several minutes passed before he heard her soft footsteps in his bedroom.

"I've brought water and painkillers. Take them before you fall back asleep."

As if he could sleep through the pounding. He sat up carefully and accepted the glass of water and three pills. He tossed the pills into his mouth, took a swig of water and then swallowed.

"Drink the whole glass."

Glaring at her over the rim, he obliged. More out of thirst than from her request.

He turned his head to check the time on his bedside clock. Almost nine in the morning. Jesus. He never slept this late.

"Lie back down," she said softly. "I'll wake you when breakfast is ready. Hopefully the meds will have kicked in by then."

She turned to leave and he caught her wrist, stopping her retreat.

"Why are you here, Kenzie?"

Her lashes fluttered down and she gave a small shake of her head. "Guilt. Plain and simple. Hoping I can get you to forgive me."

He grunted. "Not only did my men have to see their chief drunk out of his mind, but also begging for burritos. How the hell do I come back from that kind of low?"

She winced. "Ouch, I really owe you one. I'll start by fixing you some hangover food."

He smoothed his thumb over the silky underside of her wrist. Despite the pain in his head, he allowed himself a moment to really look her over.

She certainly didn't appear as if she'd come here to seduce him. The sweatpants she wore were slightly baggy and ended at her calves. They were a light pink with the year 1988 on the side. On her feet were black flip-flops, with her red toenails looking dainty and feminine.

On top she wore a black T-shirt that hugged her chest just enough to give the definition of her shape. She wore no makeup and her hair hung in two braids on either side of her head.

Right now, despite how much his dick was leaping to attention at having her nearby, he wasn't in the state of health to act on her current state of adorably sexy.

When she tugged on her wrist, he glanced up to look

into her eyes. Her gaze was a mix of unease and awareness. Beneath his thumb he felt her pulse quicken.

"Your stove is on," she murmured huskily. "I need to start breakfast. Unless you want your pan to catch fire."

His lips twitched and he gave a reluctant smile. "That would pretty much make my morning complete." After releasing her hand, he lay back down on the bed and closed his eyes. He listened to her retreating footsteps and tried not to focus on the pounding in his head. There was no way he would fall back asleep. Not with the amount of pain in his head and the fact that the sun had been up for many hours.

Music drifted from the kitchen. Dave Matthews? She must've been playing it from her phone. The smell of bacon began to float through the house.

He let his eyes close and slowly felt his muscles begin to relax. He must've fallen back asleep, because the next thing he knew there was a hand gently squeezing his shoulder.

"Can you wake up and eat something?"

The soft question had his eyes snapping open. Kenzie sat on the edge of his bed, her concerned expression hovering over him.

Could he eat? He blinked and sat up slowly, waiting for his head to explode from the pounding. Except for just the hint of pain, it was gone.

"You made breakfast?"

"You're going to want to put something in your stom-ach." She stood up and grabbed the tray she must've set down on his dresser when she'd come in. "Something hot and a little greasy. You know, the perfect hangover food."

He glanced down at the plate of food and his stomach growled. There was a breakfast sandwich of sorts with a fried egg, melted cheddar cheese and bacon, nestled between thick slices of white bread. Beside it were chunks of potato, clearly recently cut and fried. Then on the side, almost as a pretense at being healthy, there were a couple slices of oranges.

Damn but if it didn't look like something you'd order at some underappreciated diner off a truck stop.

"This looks amazing," he admitted. "Thank you."

She blushed slightly and shrugged. "It's the least I can do. How do you take your coffee?"

He picked up half the sandwich. "Lots of cream and sugar. Are you going to eat? Or let me guess, you had a smoothie before you came?"

Her laugh was warm and full of amusement. "No way. I have no understanding for people who can make anything liquid a meal. My breakfast is waiting in the kitchen. I'll grab it in a minute."

Breakfast in bed, he mused. When was the last time this had happened? Probably when he'd been sixteen and still living at home.

Despite how awesome the meal looked, he wasn't quite sure he'd be able to get much of it down. Or if he did, keep it there. He took a bite of the sandwich and gave a moan of appreciation. The combination of fat and salt exploded in his mouth in a massive orgasm of flavor.

"You look as if you're enjoying yourself a bit too much there." Kenzie entered the room again, a steaming mug in one hand and her plate in another.

He swallowed the bite and reached for the coffee that she handed him. "Absolutely. This is amazing. Thank you."

"Hangover food. Works every time."

"I suppose so. It's been a while since I've dealt with this kind of thing."

Shame flashed across her face as she sat down on the end of his queen-size bed, and folded her legs under her bottom. She balanced her tray on her lap and stabbed a potato with a fork.

"So you're not like half the guys I see coming into the pub. Not a heavy drinker?"

"I enjoy a good brandy or beer, but honestly, that's about it. And even then, all in moderation."

She nodded, chewing her food slowly. After a moment she sighed. "I've been drunk, but it's not often. Brett, I'm sorry about yesterday. I had the home field advantage, so to speak. It takes a shite-ton of whisky to get me drunk, and I knew you'd assume otherwise."

As much as he wanted to blame her, and she wanted to accept the blame, he couldn't. Not now that his head had stopped pounding and his stomach had settled. Clarity was settling in and he knew he was just as much to blame.

"I know my limits, Kenzie. I got stupid and pushed past

them."

They shared a long glance, before she nodded and ducked her head, reaching for her sandwich.

"How did you figure out where I lived?"

She laughed softly. "Actually, it wasn't hard. One of your sailors, who you must hang out with often, came in this morning for breakfast at the pub and I grilled him until he gave me your address."

"Name or description. I'll have to punish him."

Her head snapped up, panic in her eyes. Then she laughed as she realized he was teasing.

"Such a bully," she quipped and went back to eating.

She didn't seem self-conscious about eating in front of him, as some women were, but was enjoying her breakfast with as much gusto as he was.

When they'd both finished she eased herself off his bed and grabbed his empty tray.

"Can I get you any more coffee?"

He gave a small shake of his head. "I'm fine. Thanks."

After watching her attractive bottom disappear from his bedroom, he stretched out on the bed again, folding his arms above his head. Waiting on her next move.

KENZIE FINISHED RINSING their plates and set them in the dishwasher.

Her heart was pounding and she wiped her hands on the

nearby dish towel. What did she do now? Did she leave? She'd made him breakfast, given him medication. Basically nurtured him out of hangover hell. Her conscience was clean: she could say good-bye and get out.

But she didn't really want to leave. She wasn't really sure what she wanted, but she knew when she was with Brett she enjoyed herself. She was able to relax and enjoy a man's company.

And that didn't really happen anymore. Not outside of family, at least. It was a pretty big thing for her to trust a man who wasn't a blood relative. For her to be alone with him in his house just didn't happen.

This was rare for her. She found herself wanting things she hadn't wanted in so long. Her body was awake and aware of a man. The possibilities. The potential for pleasure…

Glancing down at herself she bit back a groan. And she'd shown up in sweatpants.

Real attractive, Kenzie.

"Kenzie? You still here?"

His lazy drawl with that hint of a Southern accent had butterflies stirring in her belly.

"Aye. Just a moment." She closed her eyes and willed herself not to be such an idiot, and then walked back toward his room.

His house was nice enough, and not too far from the one she shared with Delonna. It was clean, had several bedrooms and a nice kitchen. Probably a rental home, if she had to guess. A single man who moved frequently with the Navy, it certainly would make sense.

She stepped back into his bedroom and her breath caught. He was sprawled out on the bed, his arms folded on the pillow above his head. His chest was wide and defined, dark hairs sprinkled throughout.

He was so potently masculine right now, for a moment she had a brief stirring of panic as he said softly, "Come here."

Her feet felt glued to the ground, and it wasn't until he held out a hand that she forced herself to take the six or so steps to the bed.

His fingers laced through hers. "Thank you for breakfast. For coming over this morning."

"You're welcome." She sat down on the edge of the mattress beside him, struggling with the urge to bolt.

He stroked her knuckles and a tremor raced through her.

"Lie down beside me, Kenzie," he said softly. "I won't touch you. I promise."

They were only words, and lying down beside him opened her up for all kinds of trouble. But she trusted him. He wouldn't touch her unless she asked him to.

He scooted over, leaving her enough room to climb on top of the blankets beside him. It should've been weird. Maybe even a bit terrifying. Brett was larger than Charles, and likely stronger. Deadlier if he needed to be, but when her head fell against the pillow and they continued to hold hands, she had no fear.

"You don't work today?" he asked casually.

"Not 'til tonight."

"But you were at the pub?"

"Aye. I was dropping off my roommate to go to work." She smiled. "The pub is very nearly my home. My brothers are there quite often, and I've worked there since I was sixteen."

"Brothers? How many do you have?"

"Three."

"You're the only girl?"

"Aye."

"Spoiled rotten?"

She laughed, and some more of her nerves dissipated. "Oh, aye."

They fell silent again. She held quite still, breathing in the scent of him and his room. The overall masculine presence of the room.

The heat gathering inside her swelled, spreading far and wide throughout her body. She was aware of every breath he drew in. Every little maddening stroke his thumb made over her knuckles.

Moisture gathered low between her legs and she bit her lip. He was the first man in many years that she could remember being able to arouse her. It wasn't that she hadn't thought about sex or had orgasms, but generally they were fantasy-induced and achieved alone in her room.

Now there was Brett, a very solid, tangible presence lying right next to her. Awakening her body to sensations she'd thought long dead. She wanted, she realized, more than anything to take advantage of that fact.

"Do you work later? What are your plans for the day?" he asked, his voice a bit more strained now.

Maybe he was aware of the mounting sexual tension between them.

"I have none. I don't want to talk about work," she admitted, almost on a whisper. She rolled onto her side and faced him.

"You don't?" He adjusted his body as well, so they lay fully clothed facing each other. "What do you want…to talk about?"

"I don't want to talk." Oh God, she was being awfully bold right now, and it felt a bit liberating.

His gaze darkened. "What is it you want, Kenzie?"

She wanted to answer. Tried to answer, but her heart was beating so fast and the words were thick in her mouth. Her eyes must've conveyed what she wanted, because he drew in a deep shuddering breath that made his beautifully defined chest expand.

He moved slightly, so that he could cup her cheek in one hand and lower his lips to brush against hers.

She closed her eyes and tilted her head back, parting her lips to give him access to her mouth. He took it without hesitation. His mouth slanted across hers before his tongue plunged deep inside to tease and suck.

He tasted of coffee and bacon, and all sorts of wonderfully male goodness. His fingers on her cheek were exquisitely gentle, even as he plundered her mouth.

Her sex clenched as the heat exploded into a roaring inferno inside her. Need spread through her and an almost pained-sounding moan ripped from her.

Brett lifted his mouth from hers and kissed the corner of her mouth.

"What do you want, Kenzie?" he asked again softly.

She hesitated. As much as she wanted to step outside her comfort zone and beg for the whole deal, she wasn't sure she could.

"I don't know if I'm ready for sex, but I want to..." She trailed off, not sure how to say it. Her face burned with humiliation and she bit back a groan.

She felt like a bloody teenager leading on a boy. What the hell was she doing? Brett was a grown man, not some young bloke who'd be happy with only a hot make-out session.

"I mean, I could try," she said awkwardly. "If you—"

"Relax, sugar." He brushed a kiss across her mouth. "I understand, and I'm absolutely fine with taking things at your speed."

He sat up slightly and pressed his palm against her shoulder, a gesture that encouraged her to lie on her back with her head on the pillow.

"You can tell me to stop at any point, okay?"

She gave a small nod, her heart beating double time now. His mouth found hers again, his tongue dipping lightly, as he slid his hand to the area between the waistband of her sweats and her T-shirt.

Each little light caress of his fingers on her naked skin sent hot desire coursing throughout her. He made no move to go further, just kept the kiss endless and his touch light and teasing. Only when her hips lifted instinctively and she groaned in frustration did he lift his mouth from hers.

She felt the fabric of her shirt being dragged up her stomach. The cool air caressed her bare skin before he shifted on the bed into a position that allowed his lips to brush over her belly.

Her breath caught and a tremble raced through her. Still he dragged her shirt up farther, until the fabric pulled up and over her breasts.

She heard his softly indrawn breath, before he kissed his way up her stomach. His large hand moved to cup a breast through the fabric and she bit her lip, wanting so much more. He answered her silent plea, pulling back the cup and baring her to him.

"God, you're beautiful, sugar."

Her nipple was already puckered and ready for him, and he wasted no time drawing it into his mouth.

Mindless pleasure took over and she moaned, sliding her fingers through his shaved hair as he suckled her. She knew then that if he wanted her—all of her—she wouldn't stop him. Couldn't stop him. Right now, the need inside her was the puppet and he the puppeteer.

Chapter Nine

BRETT GROANED AGAINST the softness of her breast. Christ, it was like being in ninth grade again, and it was the hottest sexual experience he'd had in probably his whole life.

He sucked her nipple deeper into his mouth while cupping her other full breast in his hand. Her hips were rising and falling against the mattress and her whimpers were growing more urgent.

He had only planned to take it this far. To have some fun and keep it at the breast-play level. But seeing the drugged glaze of need in her eyes, he suspected she wouldn't be satisfied with only that.

He moved his hand from her breast and down the softness of her belly. He teased his fingers in and around the waistband of her sweats, waiting to see if she'd stop him.

Her hand grabbed his wrist, and wordlessly, she urged him to slide his hand beneath.

His dick went rock hard as he teased his fingers over the slight dampness of her cotton panties.

"Brett."

He lifted his head to glance down at her. Her head was thrown back, those long red braids falling on his pillow. Her eyes were closed, her lips parted, and she looked damned innocent and young right now. Riding the throes of passion—and about ready to ride his hand.

Damn, he wanted her so fucking bad.

He turned his attention to her lower body, watched the erotic sight of his hand beneath her sweats as he rubbed her mound through her underwear.

Her hips rose and fell against him, her thighs clenching and unclenching against his hand. He needed more. Knew she needed more. Easing his fingers back up, he slid them beneath the cotton to find her bare, smooth flesh.

Unable to hold out any longer, he delved between the swollen folds of her sex and found her slick and hot.

"Oh God."

She gasped when he pushed a finger deep into her sheath. Damn, but she was tight.

He added a second finger, penetrating her in smooth strokes that sent them both so damn close to the edge. He knew what would push her to find that release she craved, and eased his thumb around the top of her sex to find the swollen kernel that would bring her release. He found it, stroking her clit with easy, confident strokes as he penetrated her with his fingers. Her body began to tremble and she moaned, riding his hand.

Watching in almost awe, he kept thinking how fucking sexy she looked.

It had clearly been a while since she'd been touched this way by a man, and she'd chosen him. A stab of pure male triumph and possessiveness surged through him. He lowered his head and claimed her mouth. Wanted to taste her cries of pleasure as she came.

It happened the moment he sucked her tongue into his mouth. Her body bucked against his hand and she cried out, shuddering beneath him as she orgasmed.

He deepened the kiss, keeping that connection until she was limp and breathing raggedly. Only then did he lift his head and stare down at her.

She watched him through narrowed eyes, her green gaze bright with pleasure and amazement. With her breasts still rising and falling with each ragged breath, he pulled the cups of her bra back up and her T-shirt back down.

As much as it nearly killed him, he dragged his hand up and out of her sweats.

Not moving his gaze from hers, he sucked his fingers into his mouth to taste her. Shock flared in her eyes, but was quickly replaced with heat.

"Brett," she whispered. "You don't have to stop."

God, but he was tempted. Especially with the sensual feminine taste of her on his tongue now. But as much as her words said otherwise, he knew it was just the moment talking. Next time. This time had been about her. Small steps.

"But I will." He leaned down, pressing a small kiss to her mouth. "I'm going to take a shower."

Before he could change his mind, he climbed over her and off the bed, damn near tripping over himself to get the cold water turned on.

He'd stripped and was about to climb into the shower when Kenzie came into the bathroom.

His jaw clenched at the sight of her. Her eyes were still bright, her cheeks still maintaining that orgasm blush.

She didn't say anything, just pulled her shirt over her head.

"Kenzie," he choked out. "You're not helping my situation here, sugar."

She smiled and continued to strip until her curvy luscious body was naked. He couldn't help but let his gaze slide over her. The large, round breasts he'd been sucking on minutes ago, her belly that wasn't quite flat but soft and amazing to kiss. And then the smooth mound of her sex that clearly she must wax or shave—which shocked the hell out of him, seeing how gun-shy she was with sex.

Though right now she was anything but hesitant. She walked past him, completely unconcerned by her state of undress, and reached into the shower to adjust the temperature.

"That's better," she murmured.

What the hell was she up to? Surely she didn't want to

shower with him? He didn't argue as she grabbed his hand and pulled him into the shower with her.

The water sluiced down on them as she reached to cup his face, pulling his head down so she could kiss him.

He let her take control, sensing she needed this aggressive moment for her own benefit more than he did. Not that he minded. Damn. Having her wet, naked body flush against his.

Not breaking the kiss, she drew one hand from his face to his shoulders. She explored the hard muscles and he flexed instinctively beneath her touch.

But she didn't stay there for long; instead her hand traveled farther down his abdomen, before finally reaching her target destination. When her soft fingers curled around his dick he about came on the spot.

"Kenzie."

"Let me." She buried her face against his neck, while she slowly stroked him.

With his hands braced behind her on the walls of the shower, he let her stroke him into an amazing, complete and mind-numbing orgasm.

With his blood thundering and his brain starting to function again, he became aware of her laughing softly.

He couldn't help but let out a choked laugh of his own. Who knew if they were even amused by the same thing?

"I feel like I just tripped and fell into my teen years," she confessed breathlessly.

He grinned. Yeah, they were definitely laughing about the same thing.

"Me too. That was amazing." He removed his hands from the wall to cradle her face, lowering his mouth to hers in a slow, tender kiss.

She held on to his shoulders, kissing him back, her soft curves flush against his body.

He lifted his head a moment later and stared down at her. Her braids were wet and heavy, plastered to her breasts, her entire body slick and pink from the hot water.

Feeling surprisingly gentle, he reached for the soap and began a slow, thorough journey over her body. Discovering her every hill and valley without the blinding heat of desire.

When he'd finished, she took the soap from him and returned the favor. Her touch was light and confident, but far from clinical. She seemed to be drinking in every inch of him as she washed. Her eyes were wide and her lips parted slightly.

"You have a beautiful body, Brett."

He couldn't resist lightly swatting her bottom. "Thank you, but I think you stole my line, sugar."

"Mmm maybe." She set the soap down and glanced up at him, water trickling down her face. "In your letter you said something along the lines of there being no other women. That was a charming guy lie, right? Just trying to win me over? I swear I won't be upset."

That line in the letter—he'd hesitated before putting that

in, wondering if it'd make him sound like a complete loser.

"It wasn't a lie," he admitted with a brief smile, staring down at her. "On the ship, for six months, it was basically a cruise of abstinence. When I got back all I could think about was you." He shook his head, hating how he'd handled things. "And I blew it and let you go. I went out for a few weeks, determined to find someone else to sleep with—"

"Actually, maybe I don't want to hear this." She gave a halfhearted laugh and turned off the water, reaching to open the shower door.

He stopped her, catching her wrist and turning her back to face him.

"I figured out pretty quick that it wasn't going to happen. I couldn't stop thinking about you. I couldn't even muster up a tenth of the desire for another woman that I felt for you. I stopped trying," he admitted. "I figured it could only be so long before someone came along and got me all riled up again, and I'd just wait it out, but it never happened. Then you walked back into my life and I knew I couldn't let you walk away again."

Her gaze searched his, as if looking for any sign that he was lying. A combo of surprise and dismay registered in her eyes before she glanced away.

This time when she stepped out of the shower, he didn't stop her, but followed. He grabbed a towel from under the sink and started a slow patting down of her body.

"Why don't you do permanent? Not judging by any

means, only curious."

He hesitated. "I've done permanent. It just doesn't work for me."

"You've been in a serious relationship then?"

"Some consider marriage pretty serious, some not so much."

∽

THE HEAT THAT had been spreading through Kenzie as he patiently dried her body chilled a degree.

"You were married?"

"Only for a couple years and it was pretty early into my Navy career."

Why it shocked her at all was silly. He had to be in his mid-thirties. For a man not to have been married by then was more uncommon.

"She couldn't handle being a Navy wife," he continued without much emotion. "Couldn't handle having her husband being gone for months on end. She craved attention too much, not to mention craved other things."

It would be hard, but if you loved somebody you dealt with it. Kenzie pressed her lips together and shook her head.

"She cheated then?"

"Yes."

"I'm sorry."

"Thank you. I'm not the first guy this has happened to. A lot of Navy spouses can't handle it." He gave her arse another pat and then turned the towel on himself. "And girlfriends for that matter. I had a serious girlfriend before my wife, and one several years ago after I'd divorced."

Kenzie was a bit surprised to realize she held no jealousy hearing him talk about his past with women, simply an honest curiosity. She reached for her clothes and started to dress again.

"What happened with them?"

"Somewhat the same deal. One ended up sleeping around with what seemed like every guy in town while I was gone, the other struggled with depression while I was on leave, and ultimately that caused her to find comfort from another guy too. Or that was how she explained it."

"Shite, Brett, I'm sorry." She shook her head. "You told me I had bad luck with men, but it sounds like your luck with women has been just as awful."

"It hasn't been the best." He tossed the towel in a plastic hamper in the corner.

He walked past her out of the bathroom and made his way back to the bedroom. She followed, fully dressed again.

"I realized what works and doesn't work for me," he continued. "Serious, long-term relationships don't. Nowadays I keep my relationships, or lack thereof, brief. But I'm honest about it going in. I don't do long-term. That way no one gets attached—there's no pain of missing me when I'm on the boat, or me missing them. It's neat and tidy."

She bristled and folded her arms across her chest.

"Sounds a bit lonely too. Is that the way you intend to live your life then? Just occasional flings?"

"Yes," he admitted bluntly, pulling on a pair of briefs and then his jeans over them. "Until I retire. That's my plan."

"Until you retire?" How many bloody years was that?

He grabbed a T-shirt and turned to face her. "It's not as crazy as it sounds. I'm thirty-five. In three years I'll have served twenty in the Navy, which means I can retire."

"Oh." She blinked as that sank in. "That's quite early."

"That's the military for you. Once I'm living a civilian life, have a normal job, I can be the better boyfriend or husband who's home more often than not."

"Or maybe you simply got involved with complete bitches who didn't know what the word commitment meant," she retorted. "I'm certain not every Navy wife or girlfriend cheats on her husband."

"You're probably right, but I'm done trying to find out." He turned to face her, his gaze somber. "I don't want to lead you on, Kenzie. I want to be as up front—"

She held up her hand, urging him to stop. "You're not leading me on, Brett. You've been quite honest that you weren't looking for serious—and as you know, neither am I. It's just irritating to hear you write off all women on the shite behavior of a few."

"I know. I try not to, but it happens." He paused. "So where do we go from here?"

She bit her lip and sighed. That was a bloody good question. Did she want to get involved with Brett on a casual basis? Maybe he could be a good transition into dating again. Into having a normal sex life. A few times having good sex with Brett might not be a bad idea. Clearly they fit well on a sexual level, and even a communicative one.

Still, she hesitated. "I'm not quite sure. Can I have a bit of time to think about it?"

He slowly closed the distance between them and pulled her into his arms. His lips lowered to hers and he took her mouth in a slow, thorough kiss.

"Please do. I want you, Kenzie. I would love to have the opportunity to…" he paused, giving a wry smile "…go all the way together."

She laughed, loving that they could joke about this and have fun with each other.

"Aye, looking for a home run are we?"

"Absolutely. Batter up." He kissed her again. "Do you need my number?"

"I've got it." She traced a finger down his jaw, felt the stubble there. He needed a shave.

"Are you going to give me your number?"

"Not yet." She pulled her hand away and stepped back.

He winced. "Denied."

"You know where I work," she reminded him. "And I'm sure you'll hear from me soon."

"I hope so. Are you leaving already?" He moved to make

the bed.

"Aye. I have an assignment due tomorrow morning. I've completely blown it off this weekend."

He arched a brow. "You're in school? For what kind of degree?"

"Paralegal, ultimately. The past few years I've taken classes at a community college off the island, and now I'm finishing up with some electives online. I'm close to getting the degree."

"Good for you."

She didn't need or necessarily want his approval, but still a flush of pleasure ran through her at the gleam of it in his eyes. The hint of surprise and respect there irritated her a bit, though.

"I love our pub, and I've worked there since I was legally able to, but this is also something I want to do."

"You don't need to defend yourself, Kenzie. The pub is an amazing place, but it's your brother's baby. It's completely understandable you'd want more for yourself."

It was disturbing how fast he'd nailed it. And how she was starting to think about having him just nail her.

Slow down, girl. Use more than your hormones alone to make decisions.

And wow, he was still making that bed. Stretching every sheet and blanket until there wasn't a visible wrinkle anywhere. Must be that military thing. God, she'd love to see his reaction if he saw her made bed—or comforter in a clump on top of it. Making beds? Who had time for that sort of nonsense?

"Thank you." She nodded. "For everything this morning and for forgiving me for yesterday."

"Nothing to forgive."

Her lips quirked with amusement. "Don't go so easy on me. I knew damn well you'd be on your arse by the time I was through with you."

"In that case, I look forward to retribution of the…pleasurable kind."

It was a nonthreatening threat, not really designed to make her afraid, but more aroused. It worked.

"We'll see," she murmured flippantly. "But in the future, lay off the whisky, Sailor. Your head for it isn't as big as your ego thinks it is."

She only just avoided the pillow he tossed her way, before she ducked out the door.

"ARE YOU SINGING, Chief?"

Guilty as charged. It was Monday morning and Brett had been enjoying being alone for the quiet start. He usually arrived a half hour earlier than the troops did, using the time to check e-mails and read over what had to be done today. Get shit in order. Not to mention it allowed him to watch from a distance to see who, out of the twenty-four troops he was in charge of, was late or who was early.

And this morning he'd been so deep in thought he hadn't even realized his men were arriving.

Brett wiped the sappy smile off his face and turned to face Simmons, who'd come up behind him. There were still ten minutes 'til day check started.

"I'm not much for singing." Well, not usually.

"No. I'm pretty sure you were, Chief." Simmons grinned. "'Whiskey River'? Willie Nelson, right?"

Shit. Caught red-handed. "Surprised you'd be familiar with that kind of music."

"My grandpa used to sing that song all the time. Grew up on Willie Nelson." Simmons folded his arms across his chest. "This wouldn't have anything to do with a pretty Scottish girl named Kenzie and the Highland Games would it?"

"None of your business."

"Right, of course." The sailor's lips quirked. "How was your head yesterday?"

Hell, was he really taking shit from one of his men? "You know what? You should go line up."

"Yes, Chief."

Simmons must've gotten the unspoken reprimand, but it didn't stop him from laughing softly as he made his way to join the rest of the troops.

Well shit. He should've expected some ribbing from the guys this morning. They'd finally succeeded in getting their chief drunk. Only they'd had very little to do with it—

Kenzie had done all the work.

But they were the ones who'd gotten his drunken ass safely home—only after indulging his burrito craving, of course. Well, they could enjoy the memory, because it sure as shit wouldn't be happening again anytime soon.

Brett leaned back in his chair and continued to watch his troops file in. Getting ready for shift on a summery Monday morning, with his mind slipping back in time twenty-four hours.

Breakfast in bed. Luscious breasts in his hands. His mouth. A sexy strawberry blonde kissing his neck while she stroked him off in the shower.

After just over a year of not touching, or being touched by, a female, he'd come in her hand like Mount St. Helens.

A year. When the fucking hell had he ever gone a year without sex? Maybe in his teen years when he'd been single. Then there was the time he'd come close while married to Mary and he was out on the ship. He'd returned to find his wife not in the mood—only later to realize she'd been getting her rocks off with another sailor who'd been on shore leave.

Now here he was single and with no reason not to be out sleeping around if he wanted. But that was just it. He only wanted one woman and, unfortunately, it watered down his desire toward the rest of the female population.

Somewhat of a drag, really. But now that he'd had a taste of what was to come with Kenzie, there was no way anyone else would do. He'd wait if need be, but after Sunday, it was only a matter of time.

"Hey, Chief. We, uh, gonna muster?"

Fuck. Had he really been so deep into thinking about Kenzie that he'd nearly forgotten his job?

Shaking his head, as if the physical movement could rid her from his mind, he stood and went to start the shift.

BRETT WAS AT lunch, digging into a big fat deli sandwich, when her text came in.

So what are you making me for dinner? I've got a great recipe for whisky-grilled ribs. ~K

Relieved that she'd texted him, he gave a soft laugh and set down his sandwich. He was going to need two hands to write her back.

No whisky for you. You're cut off. My house. Sixish? I make a mean jambalaya.

He went back to eating, trying not to let on to the other chiefs he'd come to lunch with that the text he'd received had just made his whole day.

Not so fast, boy. I work night shift at the bar. My next day off is Wednesday. That work for you? P.S. I hate shrimp. Can you leave it out?

Didn't like shrimp? Seriously? Who the hell didn't like shrimp? She probably hated crawfish too. He'd have to convert her. She wouldn't be the first. He typed his response.

Boy? I'm all man, sugar. Wednesday works for me. I'll skip the shrimp—this time. Wednesday sixish.

By now he was drawing curious glances from a couple of the other chiefs around him.

"My sister," he lied deftly.

"Your sister, my ass," John, another chief, replied. "Who's the girl?"

Brett set his phone down, with the screen side down, and grinned, reaching for his sandwich, taking a bite.

A moment later he shrugged. "Just a girl."

"It's never just a girl." Delmar, another chief, grunted.

His phone vibrated, signaling another text. With the other guys teasing him to pick it up and check, he forced restraint and took another bite. He chewed slowly before reaching for the phone.

Aye, you certainly are all man. I've been thinking about our shower together. Thinking about it while getting myself off, actually. See you Wednesday!

Jesus, she'd ended their little texting session with the most blatantly erotic—

"Holy shit, you're blushing."

At the chortle of disbelief from one of the guys, Brett ground his teeth together, shoved aside his shock and willed the heat in his cheeks to disappear and his hardening dick to calm the fuck down.

"It's hot in here," he muttered, even as his fingers flew across the screen of his phone. Two could play at that game.

That's a pretty sexy image. You getting yourself off… I'm just out having a sandwich, but for some reason I have a hankering for eating tacos now. Maybe Wednesday…?

Silence. Minutes went by and he started to sweat. He'd gone too far. She was probably rediscovering her flirting skills and he'd dragged her right onto that filthy path she'd tentatively stepped on.

His phone vibrated and he couldn't open the text nearly fast enough.

Sorry, Chief, Taco Tuesday is actually tomorrow. We may have to stick to the sausage…you know, in your jamba-laya.

Laughing outright now, he shook his head.

You win this round. I can't tap my dirty inner man around these guys watching my every move. See you Wednesday, sugar.

He slipped his phone back into his pocket and grabbed his sandwich again.

Delmar stared hard at him and gave a smirk. "So sweet your sister makes you blush, Craven."

Ignoring their bawdy laughs, he gave them the finger and focused on his sandwich. Tried to think of anything but the mass of sexual innuendos still floating in his head.

Chapter Ten

"TELL ME AGAIN why you can't make tomorrow night's dinner?"

While leaning against the counter of Colin's house, Kenzie bit into an apple to give herself a moment before responding.

She felt the weight of her brother's gaze as he chopped a head of iceberg lettuce for the salad that would go with their impromptu dinner. After making plans with Brett, she'd known she'd have to bail on her usual Wednesday night dinner with Colin and Hailey. She'd driven to their house today to drop off a DVD she'd borrowed and let them know she'd be missing dinner tomorrow.

Of course the pair had insisted she stay for dinner *tonight*, and who was she to say no to crab Louie? Especially since she didn't have to be at work for several hours yet.

"I'm meeting a friend for dinner," she murmured, not accustomed to lying to her brother but not quite ready to be forthcoming with her tentative love life either.

Which, seeing as Brett didn't do serious, was probably a

good idea. No matter that she was closing in on thirty, she would automatically be deemed as being taken advantage of if they discovered she was indulging in casual sex.

Memories of Sunday flickered through her mind and heat swept through her body. Though nothing about what they'd done that day had felt casual.

"Do I know this friend?"

"Colin, my God, let her be." Hailey walked by her fiancé and gave him a light smack on the shoulder. "You're not her keeper."

"No, just her brother."

"Hmm, well I swear you McLaughlins would keep your little sister under lock and key if you could."

"And why not? Safety first, aye?"

Kenzie and Hailey shared an eye-rolling glance. "Safe…abstinent. I suppose they're synonymous with my brothers."

Colin grimaced and shook his head. "That was not an invite to discuss your…"

"Sex life? You can't even say it," Kenzie drawled.

"And I've had enough of this. I'll just be running out to the freezer to grab some more ice."

He hadn't been gone a minute before Hailey swung her attention to Kenzie.

"All right. Who is he?"

Not even pretending to misunderstand the question, and knowing they only had a couple minutes tops, Kenzie spilled the beans.

"His name is Brett, he's the Navy guy who stood me up but has made amends, and it's not serious. So don't say a word to my brother. Any of them, actually."

"My lips are sealed." Hailey made the zipping motion against her mouth. "Have you slept with him?"

"Not yet, but I think it's about as inevitable as rain in Seattle."

"So Kenzie and Seattle—both getting wet, got it."

Kenzie couldn't smother her giggle. "Dirty girl."

"Definitely sometimes."

Even though their friendship had only recently rekindled in the past year—after eleven years of silence—they'd slipped back into an easy relationship. Kenzie and Sarah both had welcomed Hailey back into their lives after the truth about the sordid past had come out.

Hailey had made some tough choices that had put her in a pretty bad light. With the truth had come forgiveness, and not only had Hailey and Sarah welcomed her back into friendship, but Colin and Hailey had wound up in love as well.

"So the Navy guy is back in the picture. Is he cute? Nice? Shy? Aggressive?"

Well definitely three of those. "And Southern."

"Southern. All right, well then he's got some manners?"

"Aye. He certainly does." Kenzie ducked her head, and confessed, "I got him drunk on whisky at the Highland

Games on Saturday."

"You did what?" Hailey's voice rose. "I was there—how did I miss this?"

"Miss what?" Colin returned with a bag of ice, arching a brow.

"Ah, this one *Doctor Who* episode," Kenzie said quickly, knowing her brother hated the show. "I can fill—"

He lifted his hand to cut her off. "I'd rather you didn't. Thanks."

While he went to dispense the ice in the kitchen freezer, Hailey and Kenzie exchanged a conspiring glance.

"You'll have to fill me in later on everything," Hailey said innocently.

Kenzie gave a noncommittal murmur of agreement and then deftly changed the subject.

"How's the new job, Hailey? Do you like working and living on the island again?"

"Love the job." Hailey moved past Kenzie to open the fridge, smacking Colin's butt lightly. "And I love being back on the island and sharing my sexy fiancé's amazing home."

Colin caught her around the waist and pressed a smacking kiss on her lips. "Aye, well, I was done of that long-distance shite."

"It was an hour and a half commute, tops."

"Too bloody long," he grumbled and released her, turning back to pull tomatoes from the fridge.

It was still so fascinating to watch them. Kenzie couldn't

help but smile. Just last summer Colin had loathed Hailey with a passion and had no qualms in making it known. Now here they were, head over heels in love and engaged. It was wonderfully sappy and she couldn't have been happier for them.

Clearing her throat from the emotion that had thickened in it, she called out, "You've got dinner handled. I'll go set the table."

∽

WHAT DID ONE wear if one was going to have sex?

Kenzie stared into her closet, shifting from one foot to the other.

"What did you decide on?"

Striding into the room, Delonna was all dressed up in her jeans and McLaughlin's shirt—otherwise known as standard attire for the bartender.

"I haven't decided on anything yet." Kenzie shook her head. "I mean, do I dress sexy? Do I dress normal? Do I—"

"Overthink it much? Just get dressed like you're going on a date. Focus on that much for now."

"Aye, maybe, but even when going on a date, don't you pick out cute knickers? On the off chance shite happens?"

"Good point. Sexy bra and panties, and then whatever the fuck you want on top."

"You're loads of help." Kenzie grimaced and waved to the bed. "Undergarments are already picked out, actually."

"Holy shit." Delonna's eyes went wide. "For someone who favors band shirts and ripped jeans, I never would've figured you to have such a hot underwear set."

Kenzie glanced back at the bed. The set was a combo of red lace and silk. Tiny knickers and the bra nearly sheer.

"I can count on one hand the times I've worn them," she admitted. "And never for a man."

"When was the last time you've slept with a guy? And feel free to tell me to fuck off if that's too personal."

"We're roomies," Kenzie said lightly. "And good friends. It's not much of a secret. It's been years."

"Years." Delonna blinked. "Like, that's an analogy of some kind, right?"

"No, it's a fact. After…" She swallowed hard, not letting the memory come, just trying to keep the words matter-of-fact. "After Charles, I had a hard time dating. I've been with one guy since, and it was awful. I was still mentally fucked up."

"Wow. One man in almost…"

"Nine years or so? Aye."

"Wow." Delonna sobered and sat down on the edge of the bed. "Are you up for this? You trust this guy?"

"I do." She nodded. "And actually, some pressure is off knowing he doesn't want serious."

"Really? You're not ready to consider settling down at all?"

Amusement pricked and Kenzie shook her head.

"There's still so much I want to do. I want to travel. I want to finish school. I want to get my shite together."

"You seem pretty together to me."

"I'm getting closer, but I'm not there."

"Hmm. Well I need to get to the pub. Your brother will have my ass if I'm late again."

"My brother would probably *love* to have your arse, Delonna."

Delonna paused at the door to the bedroom. "You keep saying that, but I don't think Aleck is at all interested. It's his personality. He'd flirt with a dustpan. It would be weird anyway. He's my boss."

As if that had ever stopped anyone. Kenzie let her friend off the hook, though. Aleck was a complicated beast. He went through women with the ease of using a tissue—use and discard. Though he'd never admit it, she suspected it went way back to his Scotland days and the girl he'd been involved with. Her big, broody brother, however, would never admit such a romantic notion. If he *had* turned his interest on Delonna, Kenzie would've discouraged it. She didn't wish Aleck on anyone 'til he got his heart on straight.

She changed the subject. "How is James?"

Something flickered in Delonna's gaze, unhappiness maybe, before she looked away. "He's good. Hasn't been up to the island as much. Work has him busy."

Kenzie thought quickly, trying to remember what he did. Customer service of some sort. Maybe for a cell phone company.

"Gotcha. Well have a good night at work," she said softly.

"Will do. If you do get it on tonight, have fun and be careful okay?"

"Okay."

"If he hurts you, I'll get in line behind your brothers to distribute revenge."

"You're a bloodthirsty lot."

Delonna grinned. "We prefer the term protective, but, ya know, whatever. See ya."

"See ya."

Turning back to her closet, Kenzie finally pulled down a stretchy navy dress that was a bit short, but comfortable and cute.

With her heart flipping about what would likely happen this evening, she went to grab a shower.

IN THE MIDST of dicing green peppers, the doorbell rang.

Brett momentarily froze. Kenzie was here.

Excitement shot through him, along with a healthy dose of nerves. What was it about her that did that to him?

Cursing his immediate juvenile reaction, he dropped the knife and pepper and went to answer the front door. He swung it open, a welcoming grin on his face. It slipped slightly at the sight of her, and he swallowed against the lump of awareness in his throat.

She was sexy as hell. The sundress was nothing fancy, just some kind of navy-blue cotton, not cut too low, but it clung to her every curve and ended about mid-thigh. Her hair was down, falling around her shoulders and reaching the tops of her breasts.

He traced a visual path down her bare legs to where her feet were encased in some brown-heeled sandals.

"You look amazing." The words came out ragged and low, and her eyes gleamed with pleasure.

"Thank you. You look pretty nice yourself." She gave him a glance-over before stepping past him and into the house.

Beer, not whisky—which he was thankful for. Damn, but he really liked her. She was so laid-back. Fun and playful. Sexy.

He watched her stride confidently into the kitchen, her hips swaying, and he bit back a groan. *So* damn sexy.

After snapping himself out of the appreciative daze of staring at her retreating ass, he followed after her. She set the grocery bag on the table and pulled out an envelope and set it down too.

"These are the pictures of you and your sister. It was brilliantly romantic of you to send me those and the flowers. Of course I'd never throw them away."

That, combined with the six-pack of microbrew beer and gooey brownies she pulled out, endeared her to him even more.

"I also brought beer and dessert."

"Thank you for not tossing the pictures. And those brownies look pretty amazing. You make them yourself?"

"Not quite. I enlisted child labor. I baby-sat my niece today."

"Fantastic." He started to reach for one and she swatted his hand. "I was just—"

"Ruining your appetite, and I'm in the mood for jambalaya."

Arching a brow, he stepped closer to her until their hips brushed. "Only jambalaya?"

Her breath hitched, but her gaze remained light and flirty enough to give him hope.

"Well, at this moment I admit I'm thinking about…sausage. You know, in the jambalaya."

His heart thumped and his blood heated. It was like the dirty texting all over again, but now she was here, and he couldn't resist touching her anymore.

"It's damn good sausage." He settled his hands on her small waist. "Can't wait for you to try it."

She tossed her hair over her shoulder and lifted her chin to meet his gaze. There was heat in her eyes as her hands settled against his chest.

"I'm a little anxious myself. Been thinking about it since Monday."

"Have you now." He lowered his head and brushed a

light kiss over her soft lips.

"Aye."

"I hope you like it hot."

Her lashes fluttered down. "I can handle hot."

He kissed her again, deeper this time, sweeping his tongue in to tease hers. She kissed him back, moaning softly and sucking on his tongue.

Reaching between them, he slid a hand up to cup her breast through the dress. Her bra must've been equally thin, because even under both layers of material, her nipple pebbled in his palm.

She whimpered and arched against him, her head falling back. He couldn't resist planting an open-mouthed kiss on the wildly pounding pulse there.

"We should start."

"Yes," she whispered raggedly. Her lashes swept up and her dazed expression slowly focused. "Wait, now? What about dinner?"

"That's what I mean, sugar. You're going to be on pepper-cutting duty as we start preparing the food." He stroked his thumb over her nipple and gave a slow smile. "Did you think I meant something else?"

She blinked and then thumped him in the chest. "You did that on purpose. Got me all hot and bothered and then put me on pepper-cutting duty? You wanker."

He laughed and caught her wrist, pulling her hand up to brush a kiss across her knuckles.

"Yes, ma'am, I did. Consider it sensual retribution for giving me a hard-on while having lunch with some guys."

Her eyes widened. "While we were texting? You weren't alone?"

"Nope. I was out at a restaurant, sitting with a bunch of other chiefs."

"Oh…but you didn't stop me. You kept texting. Did they notice?"

His grin widened. "Stop you? Hell, I loved every minute of it. And of course they figured it out."

She bit her lip and shook her head, looking adorably horrified. "All right, consider us even. Now show me where those peppers are."

"Deal." He moved to the fridge, pulling out the ingredients he needed. "Peppers are already half cut up over there. Go ahead and finish those if you don't mind."

"Not at all." She dove right in, chopping anything he handed her, and then watching as he began cooking the jambalaya.

"I like to cook the veggies in the fat and juice from the cooked sausage. Adds a lot of flavor."

"It sure smells amazing. I'm not sure I've ever had jambalaya," she admitted, sliding a plate full of sliced onions into the pan.

"Well, this will be your first then, and I guarantee, pretty amazing."

"That's quite a guarantee."

"Absolutely, and I don't make it lightly. Just you wait."

"And not the least bit humble," she drawled and softened the teasing statement with a laugh.

"Not even a little bit." He grinned and went to the cupboard to grab the spices he needed. "Well, hell."

She glanced at him over her shoulder from where she stirred the veggies in the pan. "Everything all right? Did you trip on your ego?"

"I'm out of paprika."

"Hmm, sounds important if I go by the sound of your voice."

"Yeah. I'm gonna need it." He shook his head and glanced at the pan full of simmering veggies and sausage. Shit. He'd made sure he'd had all the perishable food ingredients, but had forgotten to check the spices. "As much as I hate to say it, I'd better run to the store and grab some."

"Let me." She stepped away from the pan and handed him the wooden spatula. "You know what you're doing with this far more than I do. You leave me with a pan full of cooking jambalaya, you'll probably come back to find it burned and resembling a preschooler's art project."

"That sounds like it would taste kind of shitty actually."

"Quite likely. Still better than cheap-arse burritos, though."

He groaned. "I'm never going to live that down. Not from my sailors. Not from you."

"Never," she agreed.

He caught her hand as she turned away. "You sure you don't mind?"

"Not at all. I've actually got a craving for a chocolate bar anyway."

He arched a brow. "A chocolate bar? You'll spoil your appetite."

"I'm not a child, I'm a grown woman with an embarrassing appetite, who was also turned down for sex a moment ago. So I'd very much like to stuff my face with a chocolate bar as a replacement for now." She pointed her index finger at him. "Don't judge."

His mouth was still flapping as she strode out of the kitchen toward the front door. She was replacing his dick with a chocolate bar?

"Wait. I was trying to be a gentleman. I didn't want to rush you. We can turn this food on simmer—"

"Too late. Chocolate first. Sex later. Maybe."

"But you said we were even," he hollered.

She paused at the door and gave him the most fake innocent smile ever. "We are."

The idea of running after her and throwing himself around her leg had appeal, but then again so did keeping his pride.

Stupid. He'd been so stupid for not just picking her up and carrying her off to the bedroom. Manners or teasing be damned. She was clearly ready to give him the go-ahead tonight, and he'd put his jambalaya first.

Epic fail.

♒

PAPRIKA.

Kenzie paced the spice aisle of the local grocer and scowled at the variety of options.

Were these in alphabetical order?

She crouched down slightly, trying to keep her dress from riding up, and her high heels steady, as she snagged the spice she needed.

"You look good in that position."

Every muscle in her body coiled with revulsion. Using every ounce of mental strength she had, she straightened and turned to face the asshole.

Why did she have to keep running into him? It was a big island, but a small town essentially. It was inevitable it'd happen now and then, but why the bloody hell did it have to be more often than not?

"Save it for the next woman you assault, jackass."

"Ouch." Charles grinned and blocked her as she made to step around him. "Sounds like someone's bitter she never got her orgasm."

Oh God, but she wanted to kick him in the nuts. The arrogance. The complete evil in him.

"Sounds like someone is a little too comfortable giving off creeper, rapist vibes and needs to get the fuck out of my way."

His gaze narrowed, glittered with fury that was almost lazy. "Careful with the slander, McLaughlin. I was found innocent."

"Yes, well so was O.J. Fortunately, karma caught up with his arse." She moved to step around him again and once more he blocked her path.

"*I* wouldn't mind catching up with your ass. I always enjoyed your spirit, and other things." He leered at her breasts and said softly, "Would love to find out if my Highland hottie is a natural fire crotch. You realize it's only a matter of time."

Shock and fear ripped through her, draining the color from her face before it came rushing back in rage. Dimly she was aware of people farther down the aisle, discussing cake mixes, completely oblivious to the verbal assault she'd just endured.

She was tired of this. Tired of being afraid. Tired of being ashamed. Tired of this fuckin' wanker getting in her face.

"Stay away from me," she ground out. "Don't talk to me. Don't look at me. Don't even think about me. Or I swear that you will live to regret it."

"Your brother—the cop?—makes similar threats," Charles murmured, seeming completely unfazed. He leaned forward. "Haven't you guys figured it out? I'm untouchable. I can do whatever the hell I want, to whomever I want. So if I were you…" He paused, as if realizing a threat might go too far; still his gaze shimmered with lust and rage. "It's a big scary world out there, McLaughlin. I'd be careful if I were you."

Having had enough, she raised her heel and ground it down on the top of his foot.

When he hissed in pain and stumbled back, she rushed past, leaving him and the paprika behind.

Chapter Eleven

"HEY, YOU'RE BACK. Was starting to get worried."

Hearing Brett's slow drawl from the kitchen had a strangled sob of relief ripping from her throat. She strode through the house and into the kitchen, dropping the small plastic bag of paprika—which she'd driven to another store for—on the table.

Brett glanced up from what looked like corn bread he was making in a cast-iron skillet. His smile fell and concern flashed in his eyes.

"What happened?" He pushed the pan aside and strode toward her, grasping her upper arms gently. "Kenzie, you look—"

"I need you to make love to me."

"Right now?" He stared at her, as if her head might explode. "As in this very minute?"

"If you don't mind."

"I don't mind in the least," he said slowly. "If that's really what you want to do, but first, you need to tell me what happened. What's going on?"

"What's going on is I'm tired of being afraid. I'm tired of being ashamed," she blurted, tears filling her eyes.

"Why the hell would you be ashamed?"

His thumbs made gentle strokes on her arm, but they couldn't calm her.

"For years I told myself that if I hadn't been such a well-known flirt, if I hadn't slept with a couple different guys in high school, but mostly, if I hadn't flirted with Charles that night, well then just maybe he wouldn't have tried to rape me. Maybe I would've been more believable and trustworthy on the stand as a victim."

"Kenzie, where the hell is this bullshit reasoning coming from?" he rasped, disbelief lacing his tone. Understanding flashed in his eyes "You saw him at the store." It wasn't a question.

"Aye," she whispered.

Brett pulled her into his arms, stroking a gentle hand down her back. "You *were* his victim, Kenzie. Never doubt that and never let anyone else make you doubt that. He tried to rape you. You can't blame yourself."

"I know. I tell myself this *all the time*. But it's still there. A tiny voice in the back of my head." She clenched her teeth and tried to hold back the tears.

"Well kick it out of your head. This was never your fault." He cursed under his breath. "I should've been there with you. Did he say something? Threaten you?"

"He's much too clever to outright make a threat, but it's

implied. Him making contact with me in any form feels like an attack." Despite her efforts to hold it back, a tear rolled down her cheek.

His arms tightened around her. "You have no idea how much I want to beat this man to within an inch of his life."

"My brother Ian already did that." She gave a watery, humorless laugh. "He was the one who found Charles attacking me, and now Ian's a felon because of it."

Brett eased her away to stare down at her with incredulity. "Your *brother* was found guilty?"

"Aye, and there's another bit that torments me. I'm essentially the reason Ian went to jail and will always carry the label of a convicted felon."

"No. You're not responsible. Charles Richland is. And any blame you've put on yourself over the years, you need to let it go." He cupped her face. "Sugar, I would've had the same response as your brother. I might've even killed the bastard, to be honest."

"I think Ian would've if he hadn't been interrupted."

Brett stared down at her, and the genuine frustration and concern there put a lump right back in her throat.

"I'm sorry, Kenzie. Sorry for what you've had to go through, and your brother. But please, sugar, stop blaming yourself."

"I will," she agreed quietly. Resolutely. "I'm done blaming myself, and thinking I could've done something different. For years I simply didn't get involved with men because it was easier. Safer."

"Understandable."

"But I like you quite a bit, Brett, and I want to sleep with you, more than I've wanted to sleep with anyone. I refuse to let myself be afraid of that or ashamed by it."

The mix of emotions in his gaze ranged from admiration to desire.

"I'd be pretty damn sad if you did, sugar." He tilted her head up and pressed a soft, gentle kiss on her lips.

Warmth bubbled through her, pushing aside the tension as she welcomed his comfort completely. It was almost weird how she felt protected when with him.

He lifted his head and pressed a soft kiss to the top of her head.

"We don't have to have sex now," she murmured. "I was a little emotional. Ranting. You can finish making your jambalaya. But before this night is over, it's going to happen."

He smoothed a hand low on her back and then up again. His lips brushed her ear. "Well, what are you more hungry for right now?"

A shiver raced up her spine where his fingertips teased, and she swallowed hard.

Finally, she confessed softly, "You."

He tightened his hand on her back, pulling her harder against him. His lips closed around her earlobe, sucking lightly until she gave a soft cry of surprise and pleasure.

Lifting his head a moment later, he murmured, "We can eat jambalaya jambalater. Give me five minutes and I'll meet you in my room."

She couldn't even laugh at his cheesy jambalaya joke, just gave a small nod.

Slipping from his arms, she turned and made her way to his room. Her body trembled with a potent mix of need and nerves.

Once in his room she folded her arms in front of her waist and glanced around. What did she do now? Did she undress and lie down on the bed? Did he want to be here when she did?

Speaking of the bed. Her gaze flitted over to it and she swallowed hard. Already her head filled with images of the two of them and what would be happening in a matter of minutes. Her nerves should've gotten worse, because it had been so long since she'd done this.

"You're overthinking it."

She turned at his soft words and gave a wry smile.

"Aye, of course I am." She lifted her eyes and let the need that had been building so steadily inside her shine out from her gaze. "So why don't you stop me from thinking already?"

"That's what I'm here to do, sugar." His stare, equally as heated, swept over her, before he closed the distance between them.

He slid one arm confidently around her waist, and the other into her hair, tugging her head back. His head dipped and his mouth sought hers.

She was ready. Needy. Opening her mouth and drinking deep of his kiss. Sucking his tongue into her mouth and pressing her body flush against his.

His hands roved her body. Pressing lightly in the small of her back, letting her feel his swelling erection against her belly. Nervous and excited flutters swelled in her stomach and she moaned softly. The flesh between her legs warmed. Grew wetter.

"Touch me," she whispered against his mouth, tracing her fingers over his chest. "Please, Brett."

The groan he made in response thrilled her. His hand at the small of her back tightened on her dress, before he gathered the fabric in both hands and began to tug it up her body.

She stepped back, giving him room to work. The cool air in the room caressed each inch of flesh he exposed. A moment later she stood only in her matching bra and panty set that she'd spent so much time picking out.

Watching the flash of appreciation and hunger in his eyes made it all worth it.

"You're gorgeous, Kenzie."

"Thank you," she whispered.

He reached out to cup her breasts, teasing the tips through her bra. "And if this isn't the prettiest damn underwear set I've ever seen... Damn shame it's going to come off so fast."

"That must mean it's effective."

"Definitely." With a quick movement, he slipped a hand back to unfasten her bra, then pulled it deftly from her body.

Her breasts spilled free, heavy and aching. She resisted the urge to reach up and hold them. Cover them. They were on the larger side, and it was always more comfortable to keep them in a bra than let them be free. But they weren't unsupported for long. Brett moved to cup them both, lifting them and kneading them in his hands.

"Beautiful." His head dipped and he closed his lips around one waiting nipple.

Pure pleasure zinged through her blood and she cried out, gripping his shoulders as she lost herself in the sensation of his sucking on her.

Each pull of his mouth sent darts of pleasure straight to her sex, and she squirmed against him. Needing the ache to ease. Needing his touch down there.

While drawing on one breast, he rolled the nipple on the other between his fingers.

He lifted his head, releasing her nipple to the cool air and causing it to tighten further.

"God, you're already wet. Ready. Aren't you?"

"I'm still in my knickers, how can you tell?" she asked breathlessly, but couldn't deny it.

"Because you're riding my leg and I can feel how hot you are."

She blinked, realizing she'd nearly wrapped herself

around him, and had indeed managed to maneuver herself so that his thigh was wedged between hers. But she could feel no shame. No embarrassment.

"And these knickers—damn fancy term for panties, by the way—are about to be on my floor."

Her breath caught as he tugged the sides of the tiny satin and lace garment off her body, and then she was wonderfully and unapologetically naked.

"Seems you're at an unfair advantage," she murmured, running a glance over him. "You have all your clothes on."

She watched his chest rise as he drew in an unsteady breath. His gaze was focused on her body. His hand already sliding over her hip and lower to the juncture of her thighs.

"First things first," he muttered, tracing her folds. "I want to touch you. Taste you. And I don't think I can wait a second longer."

In the big picture, did it really matter if his clothes were on? She couldn't be bothered to care, not when he slid a finger inside her and she damn near came on the spot.

Oh God but she needed this.

She closed her eyes and gasped. "Whatever you want, Brett. However you want. Just, please, don't stop."

WHATEVER YOU WANT.

However you want.

The eroticism and her innocent trust in those words was

so damn sexy. Empowering.

With her hot, tight body gripping his finger, he could only imagine turning her around and having her lean over the bed. Or lifting her up and taking her against the wall.

But first things first. He hadn't been waxing poetic. The desire to touch her and taste her was foremost in his mind.

He eased another finger into her slick channel, moving them in and out, until the sound of her moans mixed with the sounds of her arousal. Their mouths fused together again. Their tongues sparred in a thrusting motion similar to what was happening down south.

But it wasn't enough. With a groan, he caught her ass in his hands, lifting her off the ground. Her legs wrapped around his waist as he stumbled them to the bed, never breaking the kiss.

Only when he reached the edge and his shins bumped, did he lower her onto it. Not quite as gently as he hoped, because she bounced on the mattress and gave a small giggle.

"Don't go anywhere, sugar." He jerked his T-shirt off, and then unfastened his jeans, shucking them off.

Left only in his briefs, he watched her wide-eyed reaction as she stared at his dick, straining against the fabric.

"You'd best let that guy out," she murmured huskily. "He looks a bit in pain."

"Not necessarily pain, but he's definitely seeking to relocate to a warmer, wetter environment."

Propped up on her elbows, her body laid out like a present for him, Kenzie gave him a slow smile.

"Well now, I may have some property he'll be interested in."

Undoubtedly. Brett removed his briefs and joined her on the bed.

"That's better," she murmured, drawing a hand down his body to curl around his erection.

He groaned in surprise, but she was already moving to kiss his nipples. To treat him to a torment similar to the one he'd given her moments ago.

"Kenzie, sugar, this wasn't the plan."

"No plan needed. Just going with what feels good."

Her delicate fingers moved up and down the length of him, and he thrust against her hand, unable to hold back a groan.

"That feels...pretty damn good."

He let her continue a moment longer, but knew if he didn't stop her, he'd end up embarrassing himself before they even got started with the real fun.

Sliding out of her reach, away from her amazing touch, he moved down her body and maneuvered himself between her legs.

She didn't say anything clever now, or protest his move. Her thighs parted, her lashes fluttered down, and she reached to slide her fingers over his scalp.

"Brett..."

It was a whisper of a plea. Almost a moan.

He answered by opening the damp folds of her sex with unsteady hands, and pressing a kiss to her already swollen clit.

Kenzie's thighs clenched and she drew in a sharp breath.

The taste of her—honey and sunshine—on his tongue, and the need to bring her to the edge had him going back for more. He teased his tongue into her again, licking and teasing the little nub until her hips began to rise and fall under his ministrations.

She clutched his head, not hiding her pleasure as she moaned and rocked against him.

His dick felt hard enough to pound nails into concrete, but his own need was on the back burner as he could only focus on bringing her the building release. Sliding a finger into her channel again, he penetrated steadily as he sucked her clit hard.

She went flying. Her hips rose and stayed lifted, while she gasped and trembled through her orgasm. Moments later she fell back onto the mattress, looking boneless and spent.

He lifted his head and smiled down at her.

"You okay?"

"Okay is not the word I'd use," she murmured, watching him through hooded eyes shining with pleasure. "Amazing. Fantastic. Fuckin' fantastic. Those seem a little stronger."

He laughed softly, and smoothed his hand up over her trembling belly.

"I want you inside me."

His breath caught at her soft statement, and he grabbed the condom he'd set out earlier off the bedside table.

It only took a moment to put it on, and then he was kneeling between her soft thighs once more. He glanced up, locking his gaze with hers, as he positioned himself to slide into her.

She caught his hand, lacing their fingers, and parted her legs wider.

"Now," she whispered. "Please, Brett."

He didn't hesitate, but slid steadily and deeply into her warm, gripping heat.

The air hissed from between his teeth and he tightened his fingers around hers.

Kenzie's head fell back, her eyes were closed, and her lips now parted in a mix of what looked like discomfort and pleasure.

The idea that he was hurting her sent a moment's unease through him. He paused.

"Kenz—"

"Don't stop." She gasped and lifted her hips. "It's just been a while, but please, don't stop."

Hearing the desperation and need in her tone, he gave himself over to the pleasure and to the shocking intensity of the moment.

With a groan, he plunged to the hilt, immersing himself in her body. And then only after appreciating how fucking amazing and right it felt, did he start to thrust.

They found their rhythm quickly, their moans mingling with the sound of their flesh connecting.

He watched her. Watched the pleasure on her face, the movement of her breasts, and then the sensual image of them joining together.

It was perfect. *She* was perfect.

A year. A whole fucking year he'd wanted this. Waited for this. It had been worth it. The realization was alarming.

But he couldn't think about that realization right now. Couldn't reflect on how this was better than any sex he'd ever experienced. How damn amazing it all was.

More.

His mind shut down and instinct took over. He moved inside her, faster and deeper, covering her body with his now as he thrust into her. Her cries rose and she pulled her hand free from his to grasp his shoulders. Her nails bit into his flesh, adding a hint of pain that made him plunge harder.

So close. He was going to come.

He reached between them to make sure she came with him. The moment his thumb grazed her clit she flew apart. It sent him tumbling into his climax.

Not just amazing, he thought numbly. When he *could* think again. But mind-blowing.

Shit. He was in trouble.

Chapter Twelve

KENZIE COULDN'T BREATHE. It wasn't because of the weight of the solid, muscled sailor on top of her pressing her into the mattress.

It was because her heart couldn't seem to slow, and her body was still in shock from the absolute tsunami of pleasure it had experienced.

She dragged in a shuddering breath and opened her eyes. Tanned, sweat-slick muscle was the first thing she saw. She couldn't resist lifting her head enough to press a kiss against the salty skin of his shoulder.

He made a murmur of approval and eased his body off her, so they lay side by side.

"Sorry, I'm sure I was probably breaking all your bones, sugar."

"You're fine." Actually, she missed the weight of him.

But the loss of contact wasn't one hundred percent, because he reached over to tease fingers over her body. Her belly. Her breasts. The tips of her flushed nipples.

Even though she trembled with exhaustion and she was

pretty sure another orgasm was impossible, arousal stirred low in her belly again.

"Did I hurt you?"

The unease in his voice made her let out a slow, low laugh.

"Please. Not at all. You were amazing."

"Careful, my ego is swelling."

She rolled onto her side lightly, glancing down his body. "Mmm. Among other things?"

He grimaced. "Pretty soon, yeah."

Well maybe, if she got some energy back, she'd find a way to seduce him into round two.

She watched him through her lashes. He really was handsome. With his light blue gaze backdropped by tan skin, and laugh lines around his eyes and mouth.

He was a man of integrity and humor. Sexy as hell, and he was single. By choice. It seemed kind of crazy. Didn't he want a family some day?

"So you're going to stay single until you get out of the Navy, hmm?"

And why had she brought that up? A bit stupid of her really. It had been motivated more by her heart, but rather than let him see she regretted the question, she forced a mildly curious expression.

"It was the plan."

"Was?" She arched a brow. "Slip of words or—"

"Intentional." He reached up to cup her cheek, his gaze

darkening. "But there's this sexy little redhead who puts these crazy ideas in my mind."

Her breath caught. "What kind of ideas?"

"Getting serious about someone again. Taking that chance."

The fact that he could admit it freely blew her mind a little bit. Didn't people play head games with this kind of thing?

"You think you could handle being a Navy man's girl-friend, sugar?"

"I...don't actually know, honestly."

She wasn't sure she could handle being anyone's girl-friend right now, let alone a man who came and went all the time. Between school, her job, and a pretty shite record with relationships—or wait, what relationships?—she just couldn't give him a straight answer right now.

The lazy heat in Brett's gaze dimmed a bit, as if she'd popped the romance and flirtation right out of the moment. Well, fuck, but she had.

Brett gave a small nod. "It's not easy. Which is why I should stick to my self-imposed rule."

She bit her lip, struggling to find the right words to say. How to hit rewind on the last thirty seconds.

"I'm going to get that jambalaya simmering." Brett rolled away, then eased off the bed. "I'll be back in a few minutes."

And clearly she sucked at romance.

Kenzie closed her eyes with a groan and rolled onto her

back. Her head sank into the feather pillow and the scent of Brett's shampoo engulfed her.

Not that he probably used much on his closely cut military hair, but she'd definitely become accustomed to the scent.

The sounds of him slicing and dicing and then frying something in the kitchen drifted through the house. Followed by the absolutely heavenly scent of the jambalaya.

More than a few minutes went by, more like twenty if she had to guess. Was he avoiding her? Avoiding the awkward way she'd left things?

Finally footsteps announced his return and she opened her eyes when the bed dipped.

"I'm sorry," she blurted immediately.

Brett slid next to her, dropping his head to nuzzle her breast. "Why? For being honest?"

"Aye." Her heart fluttered.

He kissed her nipple and it immediately tightened, lifting toward his lips.

"Don't be sorry for being honest. It took courage to say it. The Navy bred me to appreciate those kind of basic, sometimes forgotten core values." He closed his mouth over her breast and sucked, releasing the tip a moment later. "Mmm. What it didn't teach me about, but I can also appreciate, is a gorgeous pair of breasts."

Her laugh was half arousal and half genuine amusement. "By all means, keep appreciating. Well, that is if you're done in the kitchen?"

"Jambalaya is simmering and will taste better the longer it does." He tongued her nipple again. "Meanwhile, I'm fixing to keep tasting some of this."

She couldn't possibly orgasm again, could she? This soon? Her muscles still felt like pudding, and her body ached in places she'd long forgotten about.

While still suckling her, Brett moved a hand between her legs. Clearly, she was about to prove her body wrong.

He had clever, skilled fingers that seemed to know exactly where and how to touch her. As if she were the guitar he'd grown up playing. She molded to his hands. To his touch. Her body softening and rising to the pleasure, and he brought her there effortlessly.

"I'm never going to be able to walk again, you realize," she mumbled, when she could finally think, let alone speak.

"Something tells me you'll be fine." He eased upward to kiss her mouth.

When he lifted his head, she confessed, "I want more than tonight, Brett. More than a couple nights."

He stared down at her. "Meaning?"

"Meaning, I don't know how I am with dating a guy in the Navy. I don't really know how I am dating *any* guy right now. There's a possibility I'll freak out on your arse." She hesitated. "Actually, it's quite likely."

"And if I'm willing to take that risk?"

She searched his gaze and whispered, "Then I'd hate myself if I became another woman who hurt you."

He rubbed his thumb over her lower lip. "I've developed some pretty thick skin over the years. And truth be told, I don't much care for the idea of this being a couple of times deal either."

"No?"

"I like the idea of having you around a while. Not to mention we're pretty damn explosive in the bedroom."

"Aye." She wouldn't deny it. "When do you leave to go out on the ship again?"

"Not anytime soon. So we have plenty of time to figure out if this is just something fun that lasts for a while…" he paused "…or something more."

"No pressure."

"None from either of us."

"I like it." And she did. It didn't have to be a one-night stand, or a brief fling, but they could be free to enjoy each other. To do something as simple as date.

"Me too." He gave a slow smile. "You hungry?"

"For food?"

"Yes, Miss Insatiable. For food."

She laughed heartily and swatted his shoulder. "Aye. You'll soon realize I'm always hungry."

"Actually, I think I'm picking up on that." He eased off the bed and then grabbed her hand, pulling her to her feet.

"Should I put on some clothes?"

"Live dangerously. Eat naked."

"Dangerous indeed." She grinned and allowed him to lead her naked into the kitchen.

Fortunately there was only one window and the view was of the backyard. Pretty soon they were both seated at the small kitchen table, plates of steaming jambalaya and corn bread in front of them. Beers cracked open and ready for the first sip.

She picked up her fork, loaded it up with jambalaya, and then slid it into her mouth.

The mix of spices, juicy sausage and bite of some hot pepper mingled in her mouth to nearly induce an orgasm of another kind.

"Good?" Brett had been watching her, clearly eager to see her reaction.

"Bloody amazing. This is incredible."

He grinned, pure smug delight spreading across his face. "Thank you. Or, really, thank my mom. She taught me to cook."

"God bless her. And God bless Southern food." She reached for the corn bread and a moment later discovered it was equally delightful—and the honey butter he'd made helped cool the wonderful burn of the jambalaya.

They ate in an easy silence, enjoying the food and drink. Brett stood, moving to the fridge.

"Another beer?"

"Aye. Please."

He grabbed two bottles, removed the caps and returned

to the table. "Tell me what you miss most about Scotland."

She accepted the beer from him and took a long pull from the bottle. "The lochs. They were beautiful."

"Lochs? As in Loch Ness Monster? Think he's real?"

"Aye." She winked. "We were on the swim team together. You realize loch is just another term for lake?"

"Didn't have a clue, actually."

"Well, some are sea inlets, but aye."

His look turned contemplative. "I'll have to get there some day."

"You will."

"I will," he agreed. "So when do I get to see you again?"

"Are you kicking me out already?" she teased.

"No. Actually I'm kind of hoping you'll stay the night. I want you at least twice more."

"And you called *me* insatiable."

He laughed softly. "Guilty."

"I'll have to grab some clothes and toiletries from home, but otherwise, I think I can swing it."

"I get up disgustingly early for work."

"Being that I work nights, I'm usually not a morning person. So what you're saying is you'll owe me big time."

"Anything you want, sugar."

She arched a brow and scooped up more jambalaya. "I'm going to remember that. I might bring it up in, oh, say an hour."

His gaze darkened, homed in on her mouth as she ate.

"Careful, or I'll skip the brownies and just have you for dessert."

Licking her fork clean, she gave a suggestive look that was still a bit rusty to her. "Why not both at the same time? That's what showers are for right?"

He exhaled loudly and tossed down his fork. "All right, you're done."

When he plucked her out of the chair and lifted her into his arms as if she weighed nothing, she squealed with excitement. Her arms looped around his neck as he hauled her off to the bedroom.

No matter how long this thing between them lasted, one thing was for sure. They were going to have a damn good time while it did.

Chapter Thirteen

"SO REMEMBER A couple of weeks ago when I said you'd owe me big time?"

Brett glanced over his shoulder, making sure nothing was falling apart with his troops, and then murmured, "Sure do. What about it?"

"I need you to come to dinner tonight."

"I'm always up for coming, sugar. You know that by now."

"You can be absolutely filthy at times, and I love it." She laughed through the line and then quickly got back to business. "But there'll be no coming of that sort tonight. Or not until much later. Dinner is at my brother's. They're all pretty much demanding that you come to the weekly family barbeque."

That got his attention. "Your brothers know about us then?"

She gave a nervous laugh. "My brothers know when I sneeze."

"Yeah, a little protective. I remember," he murmured,

recalling her brother who owned the bar.

"I know we've only been dating a couple of weeks and if this is a little awkward, I completely understand. I'll tell them—"

"You'll tell them I'll be there. It's fine. Just let me know what time you want me to grab you tonight?"

"Oh, that'd be every time we can find a moment alone." She gave a soft laugh. "Oh you mean pick me up? Right. Six work?"

"Six—and moments alone. Got it. See you tonight, sugar."

⌒

THERE WERE MORE than just the three brothers. Brett realized this as he stepped foot into the house. With Kenzie holding his hand, he took a moment to observe the two women and a young lady lingering around as if waiting for a first peek.

"So you're the lucky bastart dating my sister." The tall bar owner approached him first—or maybe ambushed from the side was a better term.

The hand that closed around Brett's was similar in size, but the grip was definitely harder and full of warning.

"We haven't actually been introduced." His tone was lazy, but his eyes were guarded. "I'm Aleck."

"I'm Brett."

"I'm Ian." Another man stepped forward to shake his

hand.

"Good to finally put a face with the name. I've heard quite a bit about you."

Ian was the brother who'd rescued Kenzie the night she was attacked, from what she'd said.

"Good to finally meet you too. I've heard nothing but good things about you." He glanced over at the last man and then did a double take between him and Ian.

"I'm Colin."

"They're twins. I forgot to mention that bit," Kenzie informed him cheerfully. "Colin is a sheriff's detective on the island."

"Is that so? Well I can assure you I'm one of the good guys."

"No need for assurance." Colin grinned and gave his hand a brisk shake. "I already looked you up in the system."

Jesus. On the drive over Kenzie had hinted it might be a little intense with her family, but damn if it wasn't like being called to the principal's office when you knew you'd done nothing wrong.

The women stepped forward, sliding next to their men. The move seemed instinctive rather than deliberate.

"Hello, Brett, I'm Sarah. You'll have to forgive the intimidation factor from these guys. They're a little—"

"Protective. And they should be. Kenzie's a special woman." Brett smiled at the petite woman and shook her hand. "Nice to meet you, Sarah."

"And I'm Emily." The little girl he recognized from dancing at the Highland Games muscled her way to the front and gave him a narrowed-eyed look. "Are you going to marry my aunt?"

A rush of gasps and admonishments filled the air at once. Brett's mouth gaped and he struggled between laughing and choking on his panic.

She rolled her eyes. "What? I'm only asking what everyone wants to know."

Sarah grabbed her daughter and rushed her from the room, clearly scolding her the whole way.

"Don't mind her. She gets her lack of filter from me," Ian said with a grimace. "What can I get you to drink? Soda? Iced tea? Beer?" He paused and tilted his head. "Whisky?"

There was a round of ice-breaking laughter from several people left in the room, but it was quickly smothered, and this time Brett was the one left grimacing.

Clearly his whisky incident was no secret. Actually, it was possible they'd even witnessed it. There wasn't a whole lot that he remembered after the fifth shot.

"A beer would be great. Thanks."

"Me too," Kenzie called out, then muttered, "I'm going to need it. I'm sorry about that, Brett."

Hearing the mortification in her voice, Brett gave her a sympathetic look and felt his initial panic subsiding. Her face was redder than he'd ever seen it and clearly she'd been equally as uncomfortable as he had.

"She's a kid. They're practically verbal land mines wait-ing to go off at any minute. Don't worry about it."

She shook her head and sighed. "Not exactly off to a good start here, are we?"

"A beer for you both." Ian handed them each a long-necked bottle. "I'm going to head out back and start grilling the salmon. Come join me, Brett."

It wasn't a request, but a light command that wasn't so easygoing.

Kenzie's grip tightened on his hand and he glanced down at her. She wasn't even looking at him though, but at her brother's retreating back. She seemed a bit irritated, and ready to yell after him.

"I'll be fine," he promised. "Go hang out with the girls."

"If he gives you any trouble, you give it right back to him. That goes for all my brothers."

He gave a lazy laugh, not the least bit worried. "Deal."

After dropping a light kiss on her lips, he released her hand and followed after Ian.

KENZIE HAD ONLY been left alone for a moment when Sarah and Hailey showed up at her side.

"Well, not only is he a buff hot military guy, but he's nice, Kenzie," Sarah said softly. "He could've easily freaked out on Emily, but he was so cool about her awful lapse in tact."

"Hmm, yes, speaking of, when you see my niece please tell her Christmas is canceled."

The three laughed together and sipped on their drinks.

"I'm impressed with what I've seen so far," Hailey agreed after a moment. "He's easygoing, cute, and hasn't let any of the McLaughlin men intimidate him."

Sarah nodded. "Which is kind of amazing, seeing as they're laying it on him thick right now. Then again, he's the first guy you've introduced in a while, right, Kenzie?"

"I'm not sure I've introduced any man, actually." Kenzie sighed and took another sip of her beer. "I should've realized this before I invited him over to dinner tonight. In high school I was never serious enough with a boy to bring him home, and then I became some kind of petrified freak who didn't even glance at men for the next decade."

"It wasn't that bad," Hailey protested. "Was it?"

Kenzie gave a wry smile. "Unfortunately, aye, it was."

"Well, you're back in the game, and doing all right now." Sarah gave her a side hug. "I'm proud of you."

Proud. As if something as normal as dating was an accomplishment. She was just catching up to the rest of the single world.

"And this is the same guy who went AWOL for a while, right?" Sarah asked, rubbing her baby bump.

"Yeah, but he made up for it."

"Sounds like it." Hailey gave her a sly look and then glanced off the porch. "And it appears he's getting along great with Ian right now."

Kenzie followed her gaze to the backyard, which was fenced in and surrounded by trees for privacy. Ian and Brett were chatting and laughing about something as they grilled. Any discomfort Brett may have had earlier seemed long gone now.

As she watched Aleck and Colin joined the two, and soon the four were involved in conversation. One that Kenzie suspected involved more raking Brett over the coals.

But as before, he seemed to hold his own.

"Would you mind going to check on Emily?" Sarah asked, glancing at Hailey. "She's in a time-out in Aleck's sitting room and probably wouldn't welcome seeing me right now. I scolded her pretty hard."

"Of course I'll go check on her." Hailey made her way toward the sliding door. "I'm sure she feels awful."

Sarah nodded. "Of course. Awful that she was punished."

Kenzie laughed, watching Hailey disappear into the house.

"Quick, now that she's gone, did you ever hear back on that specialty cake for the bachelorette party next week?"

Kenzie blinked. Next week. Hailey's bachelorette party was *next week.*

"I...will call tomorrow."

"Ugh did you forget about the party?" Sarah tilted her head and gave her a close look. "He's getting to you."

"He's not...I just, I've been busy. We're going on a

camping trip this weekend with a bunch of his fellow chiefs and their wives. Also, school's been hectic, and—"

"No, Kenzie, it's in your eyes. Stop making excuses. You're falling for him."

"I know," she finally admitted quietly. "I am. When not working, we're together. I haven't stayed at my house in days. I'm lucky if I do once a week. My mind…"

"Is full of him. It happens when you fall in love."

"Love?" She felt heat rising to her cheeks. "Please, Sarah, we've only just started dating. He's not sure he can handle permanent, and I need to focus on finishing my degree."

Sarah's expression turned skeptical. "Why doesn't he want permanent? He must be in his mid-thirties."

"Oh, aye, he is. But, well, it's complicated. Basically he wants to wait until he gets out of the Navy in a few years before he thinks about marriage again."

"Again?" Sarah's brows rose. "He's been married?"

"Like I said, it's a long story." *And not mine to tell,* she added silently.

She glanced back at her brothers and noticed Brett slip away and back into the house.

"I'm going to take a moment and make sure my brothers aren't harassing him too much." She quickly squeezed her sister-in-law's hand. "We'll chat later, I promise."

When she arrived in front of the three men their analytical gazes all swung to her.

She folded her arms across her chest and tilted her head.

"And? May as well just get on with it. What do you think?"

"He seems right decent," Colin said first, almost reluctantly.

"Aye." Ian nodded and he gave a wry grin. "Has a sense of humor and didn't seem too distressed by my child."

Kenzie swung her gaze to Aleck, the most difficult to please and most reluctant to let her grow up brother.

"And you?"

He grunted and rubbed his jaw. "Not quite sure how I feel about sailors."

"Oh for fuck's sake, really?" She rolled her eyes. "I'm not asking for your opinion on Navy men in general, just the one I'm sleeping with."

Ian spit out the sip of beer he'd been sipping on, Colin let out a sharp laugh, and Aleck looked near to exploding.

"Kenzie Amanda McLaughlin, if your da could hear you now he'd—"

"Realize I'm a grown woman and be absolutely fine with it?" She shook her head. "Ah, drop the outraged brother act already. Beyond the fact that he serves our country—because how dare he, aye?—what do you think of *him*?"

Aleck stared at her and then glanced back at the house where Brett had disappeared.

"He's not bad."

Argh! It was like pulling teeth with this one.

"Though if you introduced him to us, it must be serious," Aleck added.

"As if you gave me any choice." She glowered at them all. "If I hadn't brought him over soon, I'm fairly certain you would've arranged a meeting."

"Aye, it was in the works, actually," Colin agreed with a nod.

Ian snapped his finger. "Oh, right, right. The accidental run-in outside his house?"

"How do you accidentally run into someone outside their house?" Kenzie demanded. "The whole lot of you are ridiculous."

Aleck finally let loose a small smile and shook his head. "We are a bit, but we do it out of love."

"God help Emily when she becomes a teenager."

"Not going to happen," Ian said crisply. "I'll not be allowing any daughter of mine to become a teenager. I suppose I should go and check on her."

"Well good luck with that." Colin slapped his brother on the back. "If you see Hailey, tell her to head out here."

"Can't be apart more than a moment. You're completely whipped," Aleck ribbed.

Colin grinned. "Aye, and that's why I'm marrying the lass in two weeks."

"And it's a brilliant move. I should check on the baked potatoes in the oven. Don't want any explosions this time," Aleck said and followed after his brother.

"He never quite caught on to that poking holes in the potatoes bit," Kenzie murmured.

"The man can't cook, though he sure as hell tries to pretend he can," Colin drawled and glanced her way, his relaxed demeanor fading some. "So on a more somber note, I meant to ask if Charles had been giving you any issues."

Had he learned about the recent run-ins? She'd tried not to mention it to Colin, because she knew he worried about her.

"No more than usual," she said lightly. "I try to avoid him."

"As well you should. I'll bring him down, Kenzie. I swear it," he muttered, anger flashing in his eyes. "I've a lead on a girl who is reported to have been assaulted by him."

Her breath caught as hope flared inside her, along with sympathy for the girl. "Have you found her? Will she testify?"

Anything to get him off the streets.

Colin's hesitation was her answer before he spoke. "Not yet. I can't even get her to agree to meet with me yet," he admitted. "But I'm not ruling her out, and I'm following up on other leads. You're doing the right thing, though, just stay away from him if you can."

"Stay away from who?" Brett joined them on the patio and slid an arm around her waist. "If it's me, I'm going to have to shoot down that idea."

The feel of his arm around her sent warmth and a feeling of protection through her. She leaned against him and let out a soft sigh.

"Not you," she hedged, not wanting to upset him by bringing it up. "Don't worry about it."

"Richland?" he guessed anyway.

"Aye, so you're aware of him?" Colin turned his focus to Brett and arched a brow.

"Yeah. We've had a run-in. Just your basic asshole rapist hiding in a polo shirt."

"Well put." Colin gave a small nod, respect flickering in his eyes that they agreed. "He's bad news. You'd think he'd use his half a brain to stay away from Kenzie, after their history. Yet he has this disgusting desire to continue her torment."

"You realize I'm still actually here, and listening to every frustrating word you're saying."

"Aye, you are, and it's a good thing. The man is a threat to you, to all women, and he shouldn't be walking free."

"I'm not going to argue with that." Kenzie welcomed the strong hand that traced lightly on her waist. "But he is free, the justice system set him free—"

"The justice system failed," Colin said tersely.

She shook her head. "No, we can't say that. The justice system worked just fine."

"Sounds like it was the jury that failed," Brett suggested.

"Regardless, it's over. It's been over, and all I can do is try and avoid him."

"He'll slip up, and when he does I'll be there to ensure this time he gets convicted for it."

Slipping up meant that another woman would be assaulted, though. The thought made her stomach heave and a chill race down her back.

She slipped from Brett's arms. "I should…go help Aleck with the potatoes."

As she walked away she heard Colin and Brett speaking quietly.

She might've been more thrilled to realize they were getting along so well, if the subject they were discussing wasn't the fuel for her nightmares.

THE DRIVE HOME was quiet. Brett glanced over at Kenzie, found her staring out the window of his truck, seeming lost in thought.

Even though she'd appeared to enjoy the rest of the barbeque, he'd sensed a little wariness in her. Sadness. He suspected it had come from the conversation about Charles Richland.

When she'd disappeared into the house, he and Colin had continued the discussion. Both committing to keeping her safe and watching out for the scumbag. Though they didn't really think Richland would be stupid enough to try anything on Kenzie again. He'd beat the system once and would be dumb as hell to press his luck.

"Did you still want to come over to my place?" He gave her another quick glance. "If you're not up for it—"

"Going back to your place tonight was motivation for me to get through the last couple hours," she drawled. "Of course, that two minutes making out in the back bedroom helped get me through too."

"Yeah, I liked that part. Except it was hard not to worry about your brothers breaking through the wall Kool-Aid Man style and beating my ass."

She burst into laughter and shook her head. "Wouldn't happen. They'd have to get through me."

When they arrived back at his place, they'd only just stepped in the door when she wrapped her arms around his neck and kissed him.

Her lips were soft and slow moving against him, her body warm and curvy in his arms. The blood in his veins heated and he grew hard not long after she sucked his tongue into her mouth.

When she finally pulled away, her lips were moist and her eyes were a brighter green from arousal.

"You really were amazing today. My family, whether they wanted to or not, liked you."

"I'm glad to hear it. I know how important family is, and especially to you."

"Aye. My brothers and da have been the only men in my life for nearly all of it. Then there was you…"

"Then there was me." He stole another slow kiss, and slid his hands from her waist to squeeze the soft lushness of her ass. "And although I think your family is pretty amazing,

I sure would love a little one-on-one time with you, sugar."

"One-on-one sounds brilliant." She kissed him again, her body moving against him in a clear signal that she was growing more aroused.

With a growl of appreciation, he lifted her off the ground, and her legs immediately went around his waist. He carried her to the bedroom and they fell onto the bed together—her denim-clad legs still wrapped around him.

Without breaking the kiss, he reached between them to unsnap her jeans and tug down the zipper.

While skinny jeans looked amazing on her, it sure as hell slowed down his process in removing the fuckers.

He lifted his mouth and grimaced. "Love how your ass looks in these jeans, sugar, but they're making it really difficult to get into your fun zone."

Through her haze of arousal, understanding dawned and she let out a husky laugh.

"Fun zone, hmm? Wouldn't want to keep you out of there."

She wiggled her hips, helping him tug her jeans down enough to maneuver his hand inside and beneath her panties. The first brush of his fingers against her warm mound had her moaning into his mouth.

He claimed her mouth again and eased a finger inside her, and this time their groans mingled. The slick heat of her body never failed to get him hard, and he closed his eyes to enjoy the feel of her around his finger.

He penetrated her slowly and she made soft moans as she squirmed underneath him—squirming not just from pleasure, but as she struggled to pull off her shirt and bra.

Finally she was free and he couldn't resist lowering his head to nuzzle one full breast. The nipple peaked against his lips and he opened to draw her inside.

"Mmm. Yes." She held his head against her breasts as her thighs clenched around his waist.

Her soft words only enflamed him more. He released her breast to stare down at her for a moment. With her coppery hair flared out on his bed and her eyes slits with vivid green peeking out.

She was stunning, and like a rare gem. It was no wonder her brothers were protective. Every man around probably tried to get into Kenzie's pants. Not only was she sexy as hell, but funny and so damn sweet and surprisingly innocent as well.

"You stopped," she whispered, reaching up to tease the buttons on his shirt.

He'd stopped only to think about how damn lucky he was to have her right now. Here. In his arms, in his bed. In his life.

And for how long?

That last question he couldn't bring himself to think about right now. Because he was starting to realize he might want her for longer than he'd expected. Two weeks now and they were virtually inseparable if they weren't at work. Even then, they texted whenever they got the chance.

How had they become *that* couple? He was used to teasing his sailors about that kind of thing, not being on the receiving end.

Kenzie kissed his neck. "You'd better come back, Brett."

He blinked, shocked out of his thoughts. Better come back. Did she mean…?

"Care to elaborate, sugar?"

"You're miles away."

Chapter Fourteen

MENTALLY. GOD, FOR a moment he'd assumed she was talking about deployment. That she'd jumped into the same thoughts he had.

"I guess I was." He dipped his head again, paying attention to the opposite breast.

If she'd been ready to offer him a penny for his thoughts, she clearly changed her mind as she began riding his fingers and clutching his head as he suckled her.

He couldn't get enough of her. Touching her. Tasting her. Knowing how easily he brought her to climax, and how easily she did the same to him.

Wanting to see her come, he worked his thumb between her folds to find her swollen clit. Her breaths became gasps, until she finally cried out and her thighs clenched around his hand as she climaxed.

"Oh God. Oh wow." She dug her fingers into his scalp and then let out a shuddering breath. "Brett…"

A moment later she fell limp against the mattress and her legs unwrapped from around his waist to fall onto the bed as well. Her hands, once again, moved in gentle strokes through his short hair.

"Thank you," she murmured. "I needed that."

"Anytime." Still bracing himself above her with one arm, he moved into sitting position and reached for her jeans. "Can I, maybe, take these off completely?"

She gave a slow smile. "I challenge you."

It took him a pinch of determination, a rock-hard dick, and a few quick tugs and her jeans and polka dot panties came off.

The site of the damp pink flesh between her legs made him unable to resist tasting the same flesh he'd just teased with his hands.

He caught her ankles and pulled them over his shoulders before nestling back down with his head between her legs. Parting the plump folds, he licked into her, tasting her lusciousness.

She gasped and squirmed beneath him. "Going to try and give me two, I see? Overachiever."

"Damn right." He licked her again, and then teased upward to her clit.

Her hips rose to meet his mouth and she let out a low groan. Even though she'd just come, it only took a couple minutes of sensual licking and sucking, before she was trembling and crying out through another orgasm.

With her body still trembling, he stood and shucked off his jeans and clothes. Just as quickly he found and put on a condom, before returning to her on the bed.

She was ready for him. Legs parted and arms open to welcome his weight.

He didn't hesitate, but covered her body with his and plunged into her.

Every single fucking time it took his breath away. Made every nerve in his body come to life with pleasure.

For a moment he lingered, reveling in the feel of her slick heat around him. Then, when her nails dug into his shoulders, he knew she needed more, and began to move.

It was amazing how thoroughly they knew each other's bodies. The signals of what they wanted and when they wanted it.

Their rhythm was instinctive now and in complete tandem. His mind only held thoughts of her. The feel of this movement. The need to take her fully and hear her cries of pleasure.

Without him seeing it coming, she somehow managed to flip them so she was on top. Her palms against his chest as she rode him hard. Her head was thrown back, red waves spilling over her shoulders and curling around her breasts. She was the epitome of sensuality.

Mine.

He tightened his grip on her hips, thrusting up into her as she moved on him.

The idea of letting her go—ever—sent a wave of desperation through him. Had him moving faster. Harder.

She moved her body just so and went immediately still, a sharp cry of ecstasy flying from her mouth.

Watching her orgasm a third time sent him over the edge as well. He groaned, taking over and thrusting unevenly as he came inside her.

Though never really inside her, he thought some minutes later. They were intertwined, breathing heavily and enjoying the post-sex intimacy.

There was always a condom. More and more, he hated the fact. They were talking about getting tested and putting her on birth control, which would be amazing. Being inside her without the barrier would take mind-blowing sex up another level. Whatever that was.

But there was more to it than that. He'd never been one to think about having kids much, and maybe it was because he was thirty-five, but twice now he'd caught himself wondering what Kenzie would be like as a mother. What it would be like to have her carrying his child.

Which was how he knew he was losing his damn mind over her.

He shifted position slightly to look at her. She'd fallen asleep, her body curled around him.

He had three more years in the Navy. That was it. Could Kenzie handle that? Could *he* handle it? Being on a ship and slipping back into that mode where he was always wondering if she would become like the other women. If she'd be tempted to cheat.

Why couldn't he have met her a few years from now? When he was close to retiring?

Every day things were only becoming more intense between them. At some point they'd have to make a decision. Keep it serious or cut it off.

Another glance at her sleeping form had his heart clenching.

Shit. He was so fucked.

∽

"HAVE YOU ACTUALLY ever been camping, Kenzie?"

Kenzie paused in the midst of stuffing clothes into her backpack and glanced at Delonna.

"No, I can't say that I have. But I imagine it's a lot of outdoor cooking and sleeping in a tent, aye? I'll be fine."

"Plus you've got a bunch of hot Navy guys going," Delonna drawled, sitting down on the edge of her bed.

Kenzie snorted. "And their wives."

"Still, you'll be having fun, and you'll be rubbing elbows with that elite chief crowd."

"Are they elite?"

"God, I don't know. Sure sounds impressive. What does a chief do anyway?"

"Not quite sure." Kenzie resumed packing. "Brett told me his official position is Flight Deck Chief."

"Oh, see? That even sounds impressive. I really do like this guy, Kenz. He's good for you."

And Delonna hadn't been saying that arbitrarily. She'd actually met and interacted with Brett a few times now. Whether here at the house or when he'd come into the pub to visit. It was wonderful that her friends and family all approved of him.

"Aye, he has been good for me," she agreed softly.

"Though, I've got to say it's weird seeing you here. You're rarely home." Delonna leaned back on the bed, propping herself up on her elbows. "You're paying half the rent, but never here. Not that I'm complaining, well, not about the rent. Though I miss you."

"I know. I miss you too." Kenzie paused to hug her friend as a prick of guilt slid through her. "Thank you for being such a good friend as I rediscover dating."

Delonna hugged her back. "I think you guys are beyond dating."

Those words sunk in and Kenzie pulled back. "How so?"

"You guys are pretty serious, pretty fast."

"We simply enjoy being together."

"There's being together, and then there's inseparable. I think sex with James is awesome, but when we're done, I want my space." Delonna shrugged. "Cuddling can be nice for a few minutes, but I'm usually happier if he goes home for the night."

Kenzie frowned. "Really? I hate the nights I have to kiss him good-bye."

"Mmm hmm. Which leads me right back to what I was

saying. Pretty serious, pretty fast."

"Maybe it's just the honeymoon phase of dating?"

"Or maybe it's leading up to an actual honeymoon." Delonna laughed, and dodged the pillow Kenzie tossed at her. "Speaking of, did you order the cake for Hailey's bachelorette party?"

"Aye. Yesterday."

"Sweet. Was it the dirty cock cake I told you about?"

"Unfortunately, no. I don't think she'd share our appreciation of artistic edible erections."

"Well, there's a bummer. But now we know what to get each other for our bachelorettes."

"Aye, and that's so close to happening?" Kenzie snorted and went to continue packing.

"Well definitely not for me, but *you* now…I'm not so sure."

"We're just dating."

"Mmm hmm. Keep telling yourself that. I gotta shower and get ready for work." Delonna eased off the bed and headed toward the door. "You need to channel your inner Girl Scout and get ready for your camping trip."

"On my honor, I will try…"

Delonna paused in the doorway and glanced back. "One last word of advice. Spoken with all the wisdom of a woman who's had her heart broken on more than one occasion."

More than one occasion? Delonna was only twenty-three. Kenzie's heart gave a twinge of sympathy for her friend.

"Please share your wisdom, oh wise one," she tried to tease.

But though Delonna gave a small smile, there was a hint of sadness in it. "If you're going to fall for a guy, make sure he's willing to catch you…"

SHE WAS IN over her head. Not even an hour after arriving at their large, shared campsite and Kenzie realized how woefully underprepared she was, and it had nothing to do with camping.

There were three other couples, with one more that had yet to show. While all the men she'd met were quite friendly and welcoming, the women had been as chilly as the breeze off Puget Sound.

Sure, they'd been polite with the initial introductions, but she'd clearly been measured up and found lacking. Then again she didn't quite have the salon-perfect hair, made-up faces and clothing that made these ladies look as if they'd just stepped off an REI photo shoot.

Kenzie adjusted her chair by the fire and tried to tell herself she was being paranoid. Maybe she felt a bit self-conscious with her hair in braids—her go-to, no-frills hairstyle—her most beat-up jeans and T-shirt with a fleece thrown on top. But, bloody hell, she was comfortable. So fuck it all.

She slid a glance over to where the men were busy preparing the steaks for dinner. They were deep in conversation, though she caught Brett sneaking a concerned glance her way now and then.

Oh yes, she knew what he wanted. For her to go and try and talk to the ladies. Make friends. Usually she wasn't too bad at it, either. Most people tended to like her, unless they were on the receiving end and unappreciative of her blunt opinions.

Still, maybe she needed to at least try and talk to them. Give them the benefit of the doubt. Maybe she was coming across just as antisocial, as they were cliquish.

"How long have you all been doing these camping weekends?"

The three turned to face her, and she took in their expressions, which ranged from irritation to boredom.

"A few years now." It was the sleek redhead, Sheila, who answered. The one in the expensive jacket and hiking boots, who looked as if she'd had her makeup professionally done.

"Well I think it's lovely that they do this together." Kenzie gestured to the men. "And include the wives at that."

"Mmm, and apparently flavor-of-the-month girlfriends now."

The words were delivered so sweetly from the tall brunette—Jenny?—that it took Kenzie a moment to realize the context of them. She inhaled slowly, forcing herself to stay calm.

Don't be a bitch. Don't stoop to their level. She repeated the mantra in her head.

She gave Jenny a saccharine smile. "You must be thinking of someone else. From what I understand I'm the first girl Brett's taken on this camping weekend."

"So far." The other, Lisa, chimed in.

Well weren't they simply a vicious little pack? And clearly Sheila was the alpha.

She had to get through two days of this. How could Brett not have realized what little twats they were? Then again, he hung out with the boys and wasn't exactly socializing with the ladies' group.

"What do you ladies do?" Kenzie asked, attempting to keep things civil.

"I'm a pediatrician." Sheila gave a cold smile.

Shite, this woman was allowed around children? Did she live in a gingerbread house in the forest?

"I'm a lawyer," Lisa inserted, her expression haughty and dripping with judgment.

Lovely.

Kenzie glanced at the last lady. Jenny.

"I am CEO of the Wilkinson household," she said in a proud, syrupy sweet tone with a Midwestern accent. "Four children, two cats and a dog."

The other ladies laughed and cooed in a nauseating display of support that was likely as real as Sheila's breasts. This lot of them made her want to hurl up the granola bar she'd eaten just an hour ago.

"And what do you do, Kelly?"

"It's Kenzie. I'm a waitress at my family's pub, but also am in school."

"You're a waitress?" Sheila murmured, tossing her hair. "Oh isn't that cute."

"It pays the bills. I'm proud of my family's pub, actually. It's quite popular." She couldn't resist adding, "I'm sure your husbands would be familiar with it."

"Which pub do they own?" Jenny asked, her face pinching.

"McLaughlin's Pub."

By the dawning comprehension on their faces and then flash of irritation, Kenzie knew she was right.

"Ah, yes. You must be part of that Scottish family."

"You say Scottish like it's a bad thing," Kenzie drawled.

There was no reply, only more fake smiles. Fuck them. Fuck them all in their judgmental little arses.

"So what are you going to school for?" Jenny asked.

"Paralegal degree."

"Oh good for you," Lisa said, with an encouraging smile that Kenzie didn't trust an inch. "We always need a few more half-educated grunts around the office."

And there it was.

"Mm. Well, as lovely as it was chatting with you charming gals, I think I'll go and chat with the guys."

Which, she realized as she strode away, would probably

just make them hate her more. Oh well, it's not like she had a chance at befriending them. Clearly they weren't open to newcomers. Or maybe, she was really just in over her head.

Her stride faltered as she looked at the group of men talking and joking by the grill. They all had that commanding presence and self-important attitude. Even Brett did to an extent, but these guys seemed to swim in it.

She envisioned the wives, so uptight and haughty. Likely feeling just as self-important being the *wife* of a chief, as if they'd assumed the position themselves.

And here she was. The new girlfriend showing up to the camping trip. Somewhat immune to Brett's importance in his career. Yes, she was proud of him and his position, but she hadn't been by his side while he made the climb. These ladies had, and they resented her presence here. Saw her as temporary.

Which, she was, right? Brett had said that once, and though he'd hinted maybe there could be more, did he really want that? Did she?

Or maybe it was as the women had insinuated. Maybe she was just the waitress Chief Craven was passing time with. Even as her mind and heart called bullshit on that idea, a tiny part of her kept whispering *what if?*

And the same question that had been going through her mind for weeks now, came back again.

Even if Brett was willing, did she want more than that…?

❦

FROM THE CORNER of his eye, Brett saw her crossing the campsite toward him.

The guys were talking baseball and work, drinking a few beers. But the tension in Kenzie's body and unhappiness in her eyes had concern swelling inside him.

He walked away from the men and met her halfway.

"What's going on? Is everything okay?" He kept his voice low.

She gave a tight smile. "Can we walk for a bit?"

"Of course." He set his beer down on the picnic table and reached to take her hand in his. His concern grew.

Once they were a good distance from the campsite, and strolling along the beach, he gave her another glance.

"What's going on?"

"Those women are awful, Brett," she said softly. "I don't know if I can make it a whole weekend with them."

"How so? I saw you guys talking and figured you were getting along."

She snorted. "If by getting along you mean turning me into a human piñata, then aye. We were getting along fine. They're catty, and mean, and I don't fit in with them the least bit."

His mouth thinned. Shit. He knew they tended to be a little cliquish together, but he hadn't realized they were that bad. Then again he spent his time with the guys and the women often did their own thing and were pleasant enough when they all got together.

Even without Kenzie's revelation, he knew things weren't working as well for him this time. Maybe in the past he'd been the single guy on the camping trips, but he'd never felt too out of place.

They'd only been here a couple of hours and already he missed talking to Kenzie. Having her at his side. The divide of women and men was pretty natural at these things, except when everyone crashed in their respective tents at night.

Maybe it was for the wrong reasons, but he was glad she'd come and asked him to walk. It gave them a chance to be alone with each other again.

"It's that bad, huh?" he finally asked.

"It's pretty bad. I haven't seen this much bitchiness since girls' gym class and everyone was on the same PMS cycle."

He couldn't help but laugh at that imagery. "Think you can hang in there at least one night? If things are still bad we can come up with some excuse and leave tomorrow."

She hesitated and then nodded. "Of course. I don't mean to be throwing a tantrum, but jeez. These women. I can only be nice for so long before my snarky starts showing."

"Let the snark fly. I sure won't protest." He came to a stop and pulled her into his arms. "We got rushed trying to pack up and get out the door, I never got one of these."

"One of what?"

He caught her mouth in a slow, sweet kiss, letting his hands knead her waist. She sighed and leaned in to him, curling her fingers against his shoulders.

"Thank you." She folded herself into his arms. "I needed that."

"Me too."

They held each other for a moment.

"Are they all like that? These chiefs' wives?"

He laughed softly. "Not at all. Some are the most down-to-earth people you'll ever meet. Like Nicole. She'll be here later tonight with Delmar."

"Oh thank God. An ally."

He tilted her chin and kissed her again. "You've got me in your corner, sugar."

"I know, or I'd probably be taking a flashlight to one of these chicks' heads."

"If I had known they were this bad, I never would've come."

"I can handle it. Don't worry about me, I'll be fine." She pulled away and slid her hand into his as they headed back to the campsite.

He did worry about her, though. And it wasn't just with the bitch wives of his friends. He worried about Charles Richland. About some drunk getting a little aggressive at the pub while she worked.

That was the bottom line. He cared. Too much for this even to be considered a temporary thing anymore.

Whether Kenzie felt the same was another story.

∽

THE REST OF the evening passed pretty uneventfully. Steak and grilled corn were served with chips for dinner. Conversation was easygoing and everyone seemed friendly enough, but now that he was aware of it, he could sense the simmering venom in the ladies of the group toward Kenzie.

It disappointed him, but more so, it pissed him the hell off. Kenzie was a good person. From what he'd seen, there weren't a lot of people who didn't like her.

And it affected the way he treated them. His communication with them had a crisp chilliness that let them know he didn't appreciate their antics.

They got the message too, because they wouldn't look him in the eye and eventually stopped trying to engage him in conversation. They didn't even pretend to with Kenzie anymore.

What a trio of bitches. He glanced at his friends and felt a little sorry for them now. Could understand why they drank a little more than they should and hung out with each other on these weekends.

So why the pretense of even bringing the wives? They likely would have a fit and a half.

"Do you want another s'more?" Kenzie asked.

He turned to answer her, but his response died at the sight of her sucking marshmallow off her fingers.

"I…do I… What was the question?"

"S'mores? Would you like me to make you another?"

"No." God. He needed to be alone with her. Now. He

leaned toward her and lowered his voice. "Think you can plead a headache? We can go chill in the tent for a bit."

"Absolutely." She winked and turned back to the fire.

Clearly she intended to take her time, because it was several minutes—and another toasted marshmallow he had to watch her suck off her fingers—before she stood and pressed her palm to her forehead.

"Sorry to be a complete wanker, but I've got the beginnings of a terrible headache. I think I'll go lie down for the night."

There were murmurs of sympathy from the men and suspicious stares from the women. Kenzie seemed oblivious; keeping a friendly expression on her face as she bid everyone good night and then gave him a chaste kiss and a wink only he could see. A moment later she disappeared into the tent.

Brett bided his time. Hating every moment he lingered outside by the fire talking shit with the guys. After fifteen minutes, he excused himself and said he was going to check on her.

"But it's not even nine. You're not going to bed this early are you?" John's wife called out, her expression displeased.

She was the redhead—clearly from a bottle, unlike Kenzie—the prettiest out of the three wives, and seemingly the most vicious. It slowly dawned on him. She probably saw Kenzie as a threat. Kenzie had her beat hands down in looks and personality.

The longer he'd sat out by the fire and paid attention,

the more he'd overheard the women gossiping about other Navy wives. It had left a bad taste in his mouth.

Escaping into the tent with Kenzie sounded like a pretty damn good break, actually.

"It's been a long day." He gave her a brief smile. "I might come back out in a while."

He stood, stretched his arms above his head, and then made his way into the tent.

Kenzie was stretched out on the blow-up mattress, watching and clearly waiting for him.

"Took you long enough," she chided, when he lay down beside her.

"Mmm. Didn't want to be too obvious." He smoothed a hand up over her belly, pushing the T-shirt up with it. "You should be arrested for eating s'mores so seductively."

She laughed, and her stomach bounced lightly against his fingers. "Ah my evil plan to get you in the tent worked."

"So you did that finger sucking thing deliberately?"

"You mean like this?" She caught his hand and pulled it toward her, parting her lips and drawing his finger into her mouth.

"Yeah," he muttered thickly. "Just like that."

She released his finger and sat up, pushing him back onto the air mattress.

"Aye. It was most definitely done on purpose. I fancied sucking on something else." She reached for the zipper on his jeans and his breath caught.

"Sugar, what are you doing?"

She paused and arched a brow. "You think people don't have sex while camping?"

"I'm not sure these guys do."

"Well, that makes them discriminatory against nature. I, on the other hand, have no problem giving you head while inside a tent surrounded by trees."

He went instantly hard at her words, and abandoned all pretenses at protesting when she pulled him free from his jeans. She moved to straddle his knees and then lowered her head, taking him into her mouth.

Pleasure rocketed through him at the touch of her tongue on his dick. He threaded his fingers into her hair and closed his eyes, abandoning himself to her sweet mouth and handing her all the power.

Chapter Fifteen

THERE WAS SOMETHING rather naughty about going down on Brett, knowing his friends and their awful wives weren't too far away. She loved having control at the moment, and even more so, knowing that he wasn't going to stop her.

He breathed raggedly as she took him deeper into her mouth and then out again, always teasing him with her tongue. His fingers clutched her hair and his hips rose, thrusting him further into her mouth.

Did she stop? Or did she let him find release this way? She was on the fence, when he let out a low groan and suddenly thrust her away.

"I can't," he growled, easing out from under her. "Not yet. I want to be inside you when I come. But first, how about fair play?"

"What do you mean?"

"I mean this."

She squealed as he flipped her onto her back and pushed her knees apart.

"Oh no, you'd best not, Brett." She tried to keep her voice at a whisper.

"And why the hell not?"

"Because I can't shut up when you do that. I make all sorts of loud, dirty sounds when you're going down on me." She gave a small shrug. "I don't want to scandalize your friends."

Even in the dimness, only broken by their small lamp, she could see his smug smile.

"Well, you should've thought about that a few minutes ago, sugar. When you had your pretty lips wrapped around me."

"Oh, aye, but I wanted to leave no doubt to your friends and their prudent wives that I know how to please my man."

"You sure do," he muttered, and then could wait no more. "So let's make sure they know that I'm just as good at pleasing my woman."

"Brett, no! I'm much louder than you, and you can hear everything through these tents."

She laughed, and tried to push him away, but the moment his tongue slid inside her hot heat she knew it was a lost cause. With a shuddering sigh of surrender, she closed her eyes and reached to hold his head against her.

She tried to stay quiet, she really did. Biting her lip and swallowing the low moans in her throat. He seemed to take it as a challenge, licking her slower and deeper. When the intensity of her oncoming orgasm grew, she felt her control slipping.

When he sucked her clit steadily, and pressed a finger into her, she was gasping and calling out his name. The orgasm that ripped through her was so intense, tears gathered in her eyes.

By the time he'd slipped on a condom and entered her, she knew they weren't thinking about anyone but each other now.

It was only when it was over, and she lay exhausted—physically and emotionally—curled up in his arms, did she hear movement outside the tent.

A man grumbled, "Usually when a chick complains of a headache, you *don't* get laid."

Unable to hide her laugh, she buried her face against his chest to at least smother it some. He was laughing silently too, and his muscles bounced against her cheek.

"Guess they know."

"Of course they bloody well know. We probably were louder than that awful country music they were playing."

They spoke quietly, so that no one outside would've overheard them unless they were right outside the tent.

"Hmm. We're going to have to work on your taste in music." He kissed her forehead. "Are you going to be embarrassed tomorrow morning?"

"No. I'll take pride in the fact that we're simply the perverts in the group."

"And we will wear the pervert badge proudly."

They shared another round of laughter, and she cuddled closer, trying to remember if she'd ever been this happy before.

Aye, there was family, but this was different. This was wanting to cry when she thought about not seeing him in a few months. Of the possibility of them ending.

She loved his slow smile and charming humor. Loved how easily she could trust him. In bed and outside of it. She loved the way she felt so completely cherished. She just…oh God.

She was simply in love with him. It was that easy. And that complicated.

Acknowledging the sudden realization both relieved and scared her. The fear being a bit stronger, and tears gathered in her eyes. She stared wide-eyed into the darkness, listening to the steady beat of his heart, and wondered how the hell this had happened. She hadn't seen it coming, but her friends and family had.

Brett stilled and shifted against her. "What—sugar, are you crying?"

"No, of course not." Oh God. He'd felt her tears on his cheek.

"Kenzie, what's wrong, honey?" He rolled onto his side, cupping her face as he gazed down at her with concern.

"I…" She couldn't hide it. It was coming out of her mouth, like it or not. "I think I'm in love with you, and I've no idea how that's even possible this fast."

His chest rose visibly and he let out a shuddering breath. And he said nothing.

Nothing.

Foreboding swept through her, tightening her heart and racing her pulse.

"And I see it's so bloody crazy," she muttered, "that you don't even know how to reply."

"It's not crazy," he rasped, holding her still when she made to move away. "It actually makes me feel less crazy, because I've been having the same thoughts."

She stilled, her gaze searching his. "Really?"

"Yes, and if you think about it, it hasn't been all that fast." He stroked his thumb over her cheek. "We met over a year ago. Maybe we didn't get together right away— absolutely my dumbass fault—but you never left my mind. And it appears my heart, Kenzie. No matter how much I wanted to stop it from happening, or deny it. It was there."

She swallowed hard, struggling to stay afloat in uncharted waters.

"I have no idea what happens next, Brett. Where do we go from here?"

"I'm not sure." His eyes flickered with unease. "I have three years left in the Navy."

Her heart sank, and she gave a small nod. "And that's clearly the crux of the matter. What do you want me to say?" She gave a small shrug. "I can tell you that I'm okay with you leaving for six months, but it's not about me. It's about you, and you being able to put aside your past enough to trust me."

He didn't deny it, instead gave a heavy sigh. "I don't trust anymore."

"Well it's a damn shame, Brett. Because I sure as hell trust you—and I have every reason not to trust people." She moved away from him, sliding off the springy air mattress and searching for her clothes.

"Where are you going?"

"To grab some water."

"Kenzie—"

"I need a moment, all right? Please." She hesitated. "Just let me be for a bit."

She was relieved when he didn't try to follow when she left the tent a second later.

Outside she noted the others had gone to bed. The fire was out and there was nothing but moonlight peeking through the trees to light up the evening.

A shiver of unease slid through her, because it reminded her so much of the night Charles had attacked her. Anytime she was alone out under the moon, she got these mini anxiety attacks.

Which was stupid, because what did she expect? Charles to jump out of the woods and attack her again?

His words from the grocery store flitted back through her head.

I'm untouchable. I can do whatever the hell I want, to

whomever I want. So if I were you…

She had been so angry with him at the time she hadn't really let his statement sink in. It was moments like this where she got a little paranoid. Took them for the thinly veiled threat they were.

But she was camping miles from home, and he didn't know that. She was being ridiculous.

A branch snapped nearby, followed by soft footsteps.

Kenzie swung her gaze to the right and saw the beam of a flashlight bouncing off forest floor. Her heart leapt into her throat, and she was ready to run, when a tall black lady stepped into view.

"Hey," the woman called out. "I didn't realize anyone else was still awake. I just ran to the bathroom. I'm Nicole. Me and Delmar just got here a half hour ago."

Relief made her a bit weaker. "Oh right. Glad you guys made it. I'm—"

"The screamer. We heard."

Oh God. Mortification couldn't adequately describe the emotion sliding through her right now.

"I suppose we were kind of awful," she agreed weakly.

"Girl, you were awesome. You were having yourself a good time. I'm glad you're here. It's Kenzie, right?"

"Aye. I mean, right." Kenzie followed her to the table and grabbed a bottle of water.

"I missed the s'mores, dammit, but plan on getting something to eat since my hubby went to bed the minute he inflated it. Lame ass. You want a sandwich?"

"I think I overdosed on s'mores, but thank you." She watched in awe as Nicole searched through the ice chest.

"You are nothing like them," Kenzie finally said.

"Like who?" Nicole pulled out some bread and meat and carried it to the table.

"The other chiefs' wives."

Pausing in her sandwich-making mission, Nicole gave a firm shake of her head.

"I'm nothing like those bitches and proud of it."

Kenzie gave a soft laugh. "I'm glad you agree that they suck."

"Those women are nasty mean. Just evil-hearted." Nicole continued making her sandwich and waved the container of meat at her. "Look, I don't come to these camping weekends. I got tired of their bullshit. But when I heard Brett was bringing his new girlfriend I knew you'd be like a shiny new target for those ladies. So I came to give you at least one person you'd be able to call a friend."

"You have no idea how much I appreciate it."

"No problem. I gotta say, I was glad as hell to hear—literally—that me and my Delmar aren't the only ones getting our freak on while camping."

Grinning, Kenzie murmured, "I think we're going to get along fantastically, Nicole."

"You seem pretty cool too. I've been curious about you. Brett's been single for a long time, and for him to bring you to the camping weekend is a big deal. Are you guys serious? If I'm prying too much, you go ahead and tell me."

Were they serious? Yes, but with a heavy dose of no.

"We're trying, but we've both got a bit of baggage," she said carefully.

"Who doesn't? Brett's a good guy, but I don't know how easy he'd be to love."

Actually, he was all too easy to love. It was getting him to trust her that was the hard part.

"How long have you and Delmar been married?" She changed the subject, mostly out of curiosity.

"Fifteen years."

"Do you like being a Navy wife?"

"I love it. Love getting to move around. Lots of people hate that part, but we're okay. We've got each other and our kids." Nicole paused to eat a bite of sandwich. "We consider it a big adventure."

"It sounds like it would be."

"Hmm. So it sounds like you guys *are* getting serious. You wondering if you can handle being married to a Navy guy?"

"I suppose it crosses one's mind when you begin dating." Marriage. They'd tiptoed around that word. Sure, their conversations may have centered around the dynamics of being involved with someone in the military—someone who came and went routinely, but no one had ever said the M word.

"You could handle it, Kenzie," Nicole said quietly. "I promise, if you love the guy enough, you can handle anything together."

Kenzie gave a small nod. "I think you're right. Thanks for the chat." She stood and smiled at her new friend. "It's helped more than you can believe."

"Anytime. And hey, the way those boys cook the eggs in bacon grease? It's going to rock your world, girl. See you at breakfast."

"Yum. My arteries are clogging in anticipation. See you at breakfast," she called out.

Even as she climbed into the tent, Nicole's words still rang through her head. How love could get you through anything. It wasn't waxing poetic.

Unfortunately, Kenzie wasn't the one doubting that theory. It was the man she loved, who'd fallen asleep outside his sleeping bag. One arm thrown up over his head, and his brows drawn together in a frown. As if he'd gone to sleep tormented by his thoughts.

Kenzie turned off the flashlight, dousing the tent in darkness as she climbed into her sleeping bag. Somehow, she sensed her sleep might be filled with similar angst. Closing her eyes, she tried to not think about where the hell they went from here.

BRETT STARED DOWN at Kenzie, still asleep and curled up in

his bed, as he got dressed.

It was Monday morning, and back to the grind. He knew she didn't have to go to work for a few more hours yet, and it was custom for her to slip out later in the morning with the key he'd given her.

Things were back to normal.

That deep conversation in the tent, the admissions of love, it was like it hadn't even happened. They didn't talk about it again. Not during the rest of the camping weekend, and not since they'd returned last night.

It'd all been safe chatter. Making food. Making love. The usual stuff. But now, knowing he was going away on detachment for a few days, he knew he couldn't leave things the way they were.

She stirred in the bed, her lashes slowly fluttering open.

"Mmm. Is it morning already?"

"It is. Sorry to be the bearer of bad news." He grinned and finished getting dressed.

"Have I ever told you how sexy you are in that blue camouflage bit you wear?" She stretched her arms above her head and ran her gaze over him.

"No, but it's about time you did, sugar," he teased, and approached the bed.

He knelt down on the mattress and eased to the middle toward her. She reached up, cupping his head as he dipped in for a kiss. Their lips met, soft and warm. Tender.

"I should probably crash at my house tonight," she

murmured, when their lips parted. "Let you get a full night's sleep."

"Sleep is overrated, but I'm leaving for a few days."

She sat up, seeming more alert. "Leaving?"

"Detachment. It's where we go out for shorter periods of time. This time, not even a week." He paused. "I'll be back by the weekend."

"Oh." She met his gaze and then gave a small nod. "All right then. I'll just see you when you get back."

He stared at her, uncertain about her response. Maybe he'd expected her to freak out a little. Complain about the time apart—even though a week was nothing. But she'd taken it in stride. Seeming more surprised than upset.

"I'm going to miss you, sugar." He kissed her again.

Her eyes were still closed. "I'm going to miss you too, but this is your job. It's what you do, and a week is barely that long at all."

Relief slid through him, but still that niggling sense of doubt. Would she be as calm and collected if it was six months? With his ex-wife it had been tears, drama and so much blame.

"I'll see you Saturday night, then? After you get off work?"

"Ah, no. Sorry, love, but I've got plans with the girls. Bachelorette party and all."

"Ah. The night to misbehave."

She grinned. "Well, not too awfully. Hailey isn't much

of a partier. We'll have to get her drunk on sugar instead of alcohol."

"Not a bad plan."

"Oh, and my brothers wanted me to inform you you're invited to the pub to hang out with them. A guys' night, so to speak."

"I see. Is that a request or an order?" He gave a slow smile.

"Well, it's a request, but they really would love to get to know you better." A guilty smile flickered across her face. "You know them."

"I'm beginning to, yes. Tell them I'll be there."

Her smile widened, and she sighed. "You're really good to me."

Not good enough.

He loved his Navy career and a year ago would've been all over the opportunity that had just made itself known. Now, he knew what was more important. What he would choose. Or more importantly, whom.

"Do you want long-term, Kenzie?"

She stilled and he heard her breath catch. Her gaze searched his, and she finally murmured, "I'm willing to try if you are."

"I am. I've located my MIA balls, and am attempting to man up for the woman who's become my world." He touched her cheek. "I love you, and don't want to lose you. If you think you can handle three more years with me serving, then I'd love to try this committed, long-term relationship stuff again."

"I can handle it. I just want you to trust me."

"I do—"

"You say you do, but I can see the fear and doubt in your eyes, Brett. I hope it eases over time." She turned her head to kiss his palm. "I've been ignoring the opposite sex for years now. Unlike the other women who've been in your life, I've no desire to go out and replace your dick—sorry to be crude—the moment you go out to sea for a bit. I want you, Brett. No one else."

The tightness in his chest eased some, and the sincerity in her words had hope and love flowing through his veins.

"I don't deserve you. You're too patient with me," he muttered.

"Aye, and patience is a requirement when dating someone in the military. So I've been told." She paused. "And so I'm learning."

He claimed her mouth again, in a deep, sensual and loving kiss, before letting her go with a sigh.

"I'm going to be late if I don't leave."

"Go." She gave a gentle smile. "Don't worry about me, I'll be fine."

"Have fun Saturday."

"I will, and I'll come over late, after the party. If you want me to."

"You'd damn well better," he growled. "All that fun and

buildup from a bachelorette party, you're going to want to burn it off with me."

She laughed. "Aye, no doubt."

"See you late Saturday night."

"Technically Sunday morning," she corrected, arching a brow.

"Right. Either way, you're mine come Sunday. Be safe."

"You too, Chief. I love you."

The words still lit him up inside.

"I love you too."

Walking out that door, knowing he wouldn't see her for almost a week was hard. But, surprisingly, not as bad as he thought it would be. Because she'd be waiting when he got back.

Chapter Sixteen

SO THIS WAS the new dance club slash karaoke bar on the island, hmm?

Kenzie glanced around the packed club and then back at the bachelorette. Hailey seemed in good spirits, even though she'd been forced to wear a giant penis pin on her chest along with a bachelorette tiara.

"You look fantastic," Sarah murmured, nudging her friend in the arm. "Ready to party?"

"You're all going on my shit list for this." Hailey poked at her penis pin. "I should've never let you talk me into it."

Kenzie grinned. "You'll have a blast. Karaoke? Dancing? This night is going to be amazing. What can we get you to drink? And where shall we go first?"

"Sprite, and dancing."

"Sprite it is, and I'd like a beer. Anyone else?"

Several of the other gals at the party nodded and made their way to the bar.

"You've got the cake, right?" Delonna asked, appearing beside her.

"Sure do. I gave it to one of the bartenders to hold. I'll grab it again when we're ready."

Minutes later, they all had drinks and were getting down on the dance floor. Without a drop of alcohol in her, Hailey seemed to be enjoying it thoroughly. Dancing—tastefully, of course—with the men who wanted to flirt with the bachelorette.

The atmosphere was fun and exciting with the bachelorette party basically ruling the small club.

It was a damn good party, and surprisingly Kenzie managed to not think about how she was going to see Brett tonight afterward. Or think about it too much. Just anytime she stopped dancing and had a moment alone, that's when she thought about it.

Of course she'd missed him this week, but it hadn't been awful. She'd kept herself busy with work and school, and had even done lunch with Nicole. Something, they vowed, that would become at least a biweekly occurrence.

And during lunch Nicole had let slip that Brett was being encouraged to put in his paperwork to become a senior chief. Which apparently meant he wouldn't retire in three years, but stay in the Navy. Brett loved the Navy. He'd told her so himself, and yet, he apparently decided he wasn't interested in the position.

And if Kenzie found it was because of her, she was going to have to beat some bloody common sense into him.

"Hey, Kenzie!"

She turned at the male voice, and immediately recognized the man. Not only was he a regular at the pub, but he was also one of Brett's sailors. He was dressed sharp, handsome, and seemed young and confident enough for half the girls here to be all over him tonight. Likely some of the bachelorette party girls as well.

"Hello." She gave him a warm smile. "Off the ship and out partying I see?"

"Sure as hell am." He grinned in response. "Actually, I mentioned to the chief I'd be here tonight, and he made me promise to buy you a beer from him."

She'd noticed the two beers in his hand, but had assumed he was double fisting to celebrate being home.

"Did he now? Well, that's quite nice of him." She laughed, and accepted the beer, taking a sip. His timing was spot on, because she'd been about to go grab another drink.

Maybe Brett had encouraged the sailor to come out and keep an eye on her and the girls tonight. More than likely actually. He was as protective of her as her brothers. Maybe more.

"Well, I should let you get back to the bachelorette party. Good to see you." He waved, gave a brief smile, and disappeared into the crowd.

"Well, now, he was cute." Delonna appeared at her side.

"Aye, he was." Kenzie took another sip and tried to figure out what kind it was, seeing that it was in a pint glass. "But you've already got a man."

"Right." Delonna's tone dimmed a bit. "I've got a man. Supposedly."

"Hmm. I'm not sure I like that tone. You'll have to fill me in on all the details."

"I will, but let me grab a drink first."

As Delonna disappeared to the bar counter, Kenzie fished out her phone and tried to stealthily break her "no texting or phone calls during the bachelorette party" rule.

Surely a quick text to Brett wouldn't hurt. Dammit, she missed him. Especially with two and a half beers in her system.

Thanks for the drink, love. I'm having a blast at Hailey's bachelorette, but can't wait to see you tonight.

"And back." Delonna appeared beside her again, a bottle of beer in her hand. "Hey, I think people are starting to think it's time for the cake. Should we have the bartender bring it out from the back?"

"Aye, we should." She took another drink before her phone buzzed.

"Read it and answer it, I know you want to," Delonna teased, drinking from her bottle.

"I'm that obvious?"

"Neon-sign obvious."

I can't wait to see you too, sugar. I've got big plans for that luscious body of yours tonight. Glad you're having a blast, but what do you mean by thanks for the drink?

How quickly men forgot. Kenzie grimaced and typed back quickly.

One of your sailors is here. He said you told him to buy me a drink if he ran into me. So I guess, technically he bought me the drink, but it's from you. Anyway, thanks!

"Ready to head outside?"

"Aye." She tucked her phone back into her jeans and lifted her gaze.

Across the room she spotted the sailor who'd bought her the drink, but he wasn't alone. The color slipped from her face as she watched another man leaning in close to say something to him.

Not just any man, but Charles Richland.

"Kenzie? You okay? Who are you looking at?" Delonna touched her arm. "You don't look so good."

Kenzie's phone buzzed and she pulled it back out with trembling fingers.

Kenzie, I never told any of my guys to buy you a drink. I didn't even know where you were going until Colin filled me in.

No. Oh God, no.

"Delonna, listen to me." Kenzie tried to keep her voice calm as she set her half-drunk beer down on the table. "I need you to get me out of here. Now. To my car, and drive me home. Can you drive?"

"Yeah, this is only my second beer and I haven't touched

it. What's going on? Are you sick? We should tell Hailey—"

"We'll text her!" Oh God, she had that edge of hysteria in her voice. She felt kind of drunk. She was never drunk on two and half beers.

Stay calm, Kenzie. Stay calm. Where the hell had Charles gone? She hadn't imagined him. She wasn't imagining feeling slightly drunk already, was she?

"Kenz, you're freaking me out."

"I'm freaking out too," she admitted. "It's quite possible I'm being paranoid, but there's a good chance Charles Richland managed to slip me a drugged drink."

Delonna only stared for a moment, before she grabbed the beer Kenzie had just sat down and sent it back to the bar, saying something to the bartender.

Then she was back and grabbing Kenzie's arm, ushering her to the door of the club.

"Let's get you out of here."

They were at the car a few moments later. Kenzie had climbed into the passenger seat and immediately began digging through the glove compartment.

"I texted your brother before we left the club," Delonna admitted, sliding into the driver's seat a second later. "Just to be sa—"

Her words ended on a gasp as she was dragged back out of the car. There was a thump and Kenzie watched in shock as her friend slumped to the ground. Her stomach twisted and she wanted to vomit with fear and panic.

Charles slipped into the driver's seat in her place, a small, cold smile on his face.

Her energy was fading. It was like she'd downed a fifth and was on the verge of passing out. She'd been drugged. There was no doubt about it now. She pulled what she was looking for from the glove compartment.

"We meet again, my Highland hottie." He closed the door, shrouding them in darkness.

She wanted to scream. Wanted to tell him he was going to suffer for hurting Delonna—oh God she had to be okay. But she couldn't seem to make her mouth and brain cooperate.

"I'm untouchable, Kenzie." He said those chilling words again. "I can get away with anything. You're still the trashy girl on the island, and I'm still the golden boy. And tonight, you're going to realize that."

Fuck you, asshole. She shouted the words in her head, fighting the darkness.

"This time, your crazy brother won't stop us. Things are finally going to go my way." He leaned toward her and caught her hair in his fist, jerking her head back painfully. "Unfortunately, I can't say the same for you."

Using the last bit of strength and alertness she had, Kenzie plunged the small knife between them. Felt it sink into his belly. Not far enough.

"Fuck! You fucking *bitch*." His sharp hiss of pain hit her ears the same moment his palm did her cheek.

The blow sent her head sideways and she saw stars. She heard him start her car and rev the engine. The drug was starting to take hold, and she knew any fight left in her was gone. The drug was pulling her under.

Despite his confidence otherwise, she knew he'd be convicted this time. There was too much evidence, too many witnesses about. Even knowing that, it didn't help the sickening despondency she felt in knowing what was about to happen.

Charles Richland would finally get what he wanted.

Chapter Seventeen

"SO HOW WAS the camping trip with Kenzie last weekend? Likely challenging, as she's never camped in her life."

Brett finished chewing his bite of burger and gave Colin a brief smile.

He'd joined the McLaughlin men at their pub. Aleck was off work for the evening, as were Ian and Colin. The four of them sat around talking while the women were at the bachelorette party.

"It was pretty good, and your sister did great." It was an absent, brief reply, but all he could offer Kenzie's brother at the moment.

His mind was elsewhere. He was focusing on the series of texts he'd just exchanged with Kenzie. Was one of his sailors hitting on her? Using him for an excuse to buy her a drink? It didn't make sense, and he sure as hell couldn't see that happening.

They knew better than to make a move on their chief's woman.

"Kenzie seems to like you quite a bit," Aleck said casually. "I'm not sure how I feel about that."

"You'll deal with it." For a moment, he was able to feel a bit of amusement instead of unease. "She's a grown woman."

"Aye, she is. You hurt her, and you'll learn quickly I'm not a man to have as an enemy."

"Ah for fuck's sake, Aleck, give it a rest," Ian drawled. "We all love Kenzie, and this bloke here is right decent. We all know it. Even if we can't bring ourselves to acknowledge our baby sister is a legitimate adult now."

"Well who fookin' gave her permission to do that?" Aleck grumbled. "My apologies, Brett. My brothers are right. You're a good guy, and I wish you the best with my sister." He paused. "But as I said, if you break her heart, we break yours. Literally."

Ian and Colin nodded, both joining in with a light-hearted round of "Aye."

"Deal."

He couldn't help but check his phone again, seeing if Kenzie had texted back. There was nothing.

A ball of unease was gathering in his stomach, and premonition was setting in that something wasn't right. That Kenzie might be in trouble.

He quickly typed out a text.

Kenzie, sugar, text me back and let me know you're okay. I'm starting to worry.

"Ah, see that? They can't even keep from texting all night," Colin ribbed. "You're in just as deep as she is."

Brett set down the phone and then met Colin's gaze squarely. "I love your sister. There's not a damn thing I wouldn't do for her."

That ended all laughter and jesting, and all three of the brothers watched him with a deeper consideration. Appreciation maybe.

"Well, knowing Kenzie, I'm fairly sure she feels the same," Ian finally murmured. "I wish you both only the best."

"Thanks, I appreciate it." He checked his phone and bit back a curse. "And I don't mean to be distracted with texting her, but guys, I gotta be honest. I'm a little worried."

"About Kenzie?" Colin paused in the midst of grabbing his burger. "What's going on?"

"She texted a while ago thanking me for a drink she thinks I had someone buy her."

"Did you?" Ian's tone sharpened.

"No, and I told her that and she hasn't texted back since."

A phone buzzed, and Brett's hopes momentarily flared, until he realized it wasn't his.

Aleck pulled out his and checked whatever message had come in. As Brett watched, tension visibly took over the man's body and his mouth slashed into a grim line.

He shoved back his chair. "We need to get to that club.

Now."

No questions were asked as they all rushed from the pub. They knew it pertained to Kenzie. It was only in Brett's car, when they were driving over there, did the details start coming out.

"Was it Kenzie?" Ian asked.

"No. It was Delonna. Kenzie thinks her drink was spiked. She saw Richland in the restaurant. Could be a coincidence, but I'm not taking any chances."

Son of a bitch. He'd gotten to her. Brett's fingers curled around the steering wheel and fear sent blood pounding through his veins.

"Dammit," Aleck muttered grimly, "now Delonna's not answering her texts either."

They were just pulling into the club when Brett spotted the slumped body on the ground.

Brett slowed the car. Ice raced through him as he recognized the form.

"Oh fook, it's Delonna," Aleck said thickly, and jumped out of the car. Colin was right behind him.

In the rearview he watched Aleck scoop her limp body up into his arms and rush inside the club.

"There goes Kenzie's car," Ian shouted beside him. "Follow it."

Brett floored the car, following the taillights disappearing out of the parking lot. They couldn't lose them. If they lost them... No, he refused to contemplate it. Ian was already on the phone with 911.

In his headlights he could tell it was a male driving the car, definitely not Kenzie.

He brought his car right up to hers, riding her bumper, flashing his lights. The bastard had better pull over if he had any sense.

The car swerved to make a sharp turn, clearly trying to lose him. But Charles was driving too fast, and the wheels came up on the left side.

"Ah fuck, they're going to crash!" Brett shouted.

Sure enough the car was on all fours again, but now completely out of control. It veered off the road and into a small fence on someone's property.

As far as crashes went, it wasn't too terrifying to watch and definitely looked survivable.

Brett and Ian were out of the car and sprinting toward them.

"You get Kenzie free," Ian shouted. "I'm going to fuckin' kill the bastard this time."

As much as Brett wanted to be the one to take out the guy, ensuring Kenzie's safety was definitely his number one priority. He tugged open the passenger door, and she practically fell out and into his arms. She was clearly unconscious as he moved her away from the vehicle.

Sirens sounded in the distance and Brett knew a neighbor had probably called in the accident. From the corner of his eye he watched Ian drag Richland from the car, and deliver a sharp punch that snapped the man's head back.

He laid Kenzie down in the grass, grabbing her wrist to check her pulse, all while listening for more sounds of an ass kicking that Richland so thoroughly deserved. But there was nothing but silence and the distant sounds of sirens.

He threw another glance Ian's way, and found him pinning down Kenzie's attacker, but throwing no more punches.

"You okay over there?" Brett called out.

"We're good. I've just realized I'm not going to risk going to jail again for this piece of shit," Ian shouted. "How's my sister?"

"Alive and unconscious. No doubt about it, she's been drugged."

"Well it looks like Kenzie's got a bit of fight herself," Ian called out. "This fucker looks like he has a stab wound. Right here."

There was the sound of another punch, and a gasp of pain from Richland.

"Couldn't resist one more in the belly," Ian called out grimly.

The police and paramedics arrived on the scene. Doors slammed, people swarmed about.

All too soon, Brett had to let go of Kenzie so she could be taken to the hospital to be checked out. More importantly, to have a urine sample taken to find traces of a date rape drug before it was out of her system.

Richland was swearing up a storm, complaining about

being stabbed, and demanding a lawyer as he was read his rights and arrested.

‍◌

A WHILE LATER, Ian approached and asked, "Are you heading to the hospital?"

Brett nodded. "Yeah, but first I need to make a quick stop at the club to take care of business."

"I'll drive Kenzie's car to the hospital and meet you there."

"Thanks. I appreciate it."

The whole drive back to the club, Brett told himself Kenzie was going to be all right. They'd gotten to her in time. Still, there was the constant niggling *what if they hadn't* that kept racing through his head.

That son of a bitch would have succeeded in raping her this time, thinking he'd get off free as a bird. Just like he had last time.

She's okay. He repeated the mantra in his head as he strode into the club.

There were still people dancing, having fun, but then there was Hailey and her bachelorette group gathered in a side room, talking seriously.

"Did you find her?" Hailey rushed out as she spotted him.

"Yes. She's fine, but on her way to the hospital right now."

Hailey covered her mouth with her hand—tears gathering in her eyes. "Oh thank God."

Aleck glanced up from where he knelt beside Delonna, and gave Brett an appreciative, grateful nod.

Brett nodded back and then glanced at Delonna. "She okay?"

"We're hoping so."

"Head wounds bleed a lot. She'll probably be fine, but we'll be taking her over to the hospital in a minute." One of the two paramedics beside her glanced up at Aleck. "You family? Boyfriend?"

"Friends," Aleck answered flatly. "She's an employee at my pub."

Brett moved on, letting them take over the questions and help Delonna. With his concern for Delonna satisfied, he made his way around the club, searching for a familiar face.

He found the petty officer on the dance floor, grinding against a drunken brunette. It was the same guy he always had to pull off girls in the pub or bars for being too aggressive. The same guy who often showed up late to muster.

The petty officer's gaze lifted just then and landed on Brett. His eyes went wide and the blood visibly drained from his face.

Brett strode forward, his jaw clenching.

"Chief—*oof*." The sailor's head snapped back from the solid punch Brett delivered.

"If I were you, I wouldn't even show up on Monday,"

Brett warned. "Because I'm going to do everything in my power to see your ass dishonorably discharged."

Brett turned and strode away, not waiting for any kind of response from the piece of shit. With that out of the way, his priority once again became Kenzie. His chest was tight and adrenaline had him near shaking.

He'd be there when she woke up. Just like he'd be there for her the rest of her life.

What had happened tonight only reaffirmed that Kenzie meant everything to him.

And from now on, with every breath he took, he would make sure she knew it.

✍

"HOW ARE YOU feeling?"

Kenzie opened her eyes and was relieved that the hangover-from-hell symptoms were nearly gone.

Brett sat on the edge of his couch, where she was resting; his new expression seemed to be one of constant concern.

"Hey you," she said softly. "I'm doing all right. I just wanted to say, that if this is at all how your hangover was after the Highland Games, then I'm even more sorry."

He laughed softly and caught her hand in his, rubbing a thumb over her knuckles.

"I'm pretty sure yours is worse."

"Yeah, well, I'm not sorry for it," she murmured. "This will sound absolutely crazy, and it is, but I'm almost glad

Charles did this."

He looked stricken. "Kenzie…"

"I know, like I said it sounds crazy, but now he can't do this to any other women. And I'm certain there've been others, Brett. From what Colin told me, they're coming out of the woodwork to testify now that they've heard what happened to me again. He's going to jail this time."

"Yeah, he really is. No way around it. Not to mention your urine came up positive for a type of date rape drug." He paused. "But, Kenzie, I still wish he hadn't tried this. If we hadn't gotten to you in time…"

"Aye. I know what would have happened," she said softly. "And I'm glad as fuck that you *did* get there on time."

"I was out of my mind with fear. With panic." He sat down on the couch and pulled her into his lap.

She pressed her cheek against his chest, listening to his heart.

"I love you so damn much, Kenzie. I'll do everything I can to protect you from here on out."

"I love you too, and you've already done a pretty fantastic job at keeping me safe, Chief." She cupped his cheek and pressed a soft kiss against his lips. "Hmm. Or I kind of like the sound of Senior Chief."

He stiffened against her, his gaze wary. "I'm not sure how you heard about that, sugar, but don't worry about it. I'm not putting in the paperwork to try for it."

"And why the hell not?" she demanded. "You love the Navy. You've told me as much."

He hesitated. "I do. But becoming a senior chief means I don't retire in three years."

"Oh, aye, I can see why you'd hate having job security."

His lips twitched. "It means there's a chance I'd have to move again, and if we get married you'd be coming with me."

Married. Oh God, he'd mentioned it. Her heart fluttered and happiness jolted through her, making her extra awake and giddy.

"Well I happen to love the idea of relocating," she said lightly.

"Kenzie." He hesitated. "You'd be leaving your family. Your brothers."

"My brothers will be just fine," she drawled, toying with the buttons on his shirt. "And it's not as if we can't come back here when you retire. Or put in orders to get stationed here again if you do relocate."

"You're figuring out how this whole Navy thing works, aren't you?"

"I've bonded with Nicole and she's filled me in."

"Have you now? Good. I'm glad to hear it." He paused and tilted his head, giving her an inquiring look. "So you didn't freak out, or say anything about me mentioning marriage."

"And why should I? I'm actually quite interested in this open position you have for a Mrs. Craven," she said, never one to mince words or play games.

His gaze darkened, with heat and with a tenderness that

she'd come to realize about him.

"Is that so? Then will you marry me, Kenzie? Because I think you'd be perfect for the job."

Her heart swelled and her eyes filled with tears. "Aye, of course I will. We can go down to the courthouse—"

"You think I have a death wish?" Brett demanded, horror on his face. "Your brothers would have me shot."

He had a point there. "Aye, you're right. My parents too. They'll want to come over from Edinburgh to meet you and attend."

"My family will come up from Louisiana. Though they practically know you by now since I've talked about you so much." He grinned and kissed her. "Maybe we could do a small, family-and-friends ceremony down on the beach. Bring in some flowers, and I know this great quartet—"

"Flowers? Quartet? The beach?" Kenzie gave a slow smile. "I do believe you're a romantic, Chief."

He pulled her fully onto his lap and gave a low, sexy laugh. "Well one of us has to be."

"Well, you'll just have to teach me."

"I like teaching you things, sugar." His tone dropped to an intimate, deep level.

All the sensual things they'd done together flitted through her head and she smiled.

"I like that too. Maybe we should try again right now."

"Now?"

"Oh, aye." And she lifted her head for the kiss he was already leaning down to take.

Chapter Eighteen

THE DOORBELL WAS ringing.

Delonna groaned. Dammit. She should really get up and get it. But that meant getting out of bed and throwing on a bathrobe.

Unless, wait a minute. He was here!

She flung herself out of bed, ignoring the pounding in her head as she searched for her robe. It wasn't anywhere in sight, and dammit if she wanted to keep listening to that doorbell ring.

Besides, boy-short panties and a tank top were hardly scandalous when your boyfriend had seen you naked on multiple occasions. James was a few days overdue for showing up, but she'd known he'd come eventually.

Delonna glanced through the peephole, saw the male chest, and opened the door, a seductive smile on her face. Well, as seductive as anyone recovering from a disgusting head wound could be.

Her smile faded and she blinked in dismay.

"Hello, luv."

Not James, but her boss. Aleck was on her doorstep, while she stood there embarrassingly underdressed, with a stupid look on her face.

"Heeeey, boss boy." And didn't she feel like an idiot. "Kenzie isn't here right now. She's over at Brett's."

His eyes widened for a moment as he took in her appearance, before his gaze snapped back up to eye level.

"Aye. Figured as much. I came to see you, actually." His smile seemed a little strained now. "Can I come in?"

"Umm, sure."

She needed to find some pants. And like five minutes ago. "Sorry about the lack of clothes, I totally didn't realize it was you on that side of the door."

"Clearly."

Six foot five of pure male sexiness stepped past her and into her house, carrying what looked like a box of chocolates. She closed the door behind him, trying to figure out why her pulse was going a little bananas.

Why was he here?

"Let me, um, find some shorts or something." She averted her gaze and dashed past him to her bedroom.

When she came back out a few minutes later, denim shorts now covering at least half of her thighs, he was looking at the pictures on the wall.

"You gals have done wonders with this place."

"Kenzie's hardly here. I'm pretty sure she'll be moving out soon anyway. They're beyond serious."

"Aye, they are." He turned to face her. "And you and your bloke. Are you two serious?"

She blinked, taken aback by the left-field question. He stared at her, concern and something else in those vividly green eyes. It became almost hard to breathe, and she definitely couldn't look away.

"I...I don't know." She'd been home from the hospital for two days. James hadn't called. Hadn't visited. Just a text to make sure she was okay.

"Sorry, that was a bit out of line." His gaze darkened.

She blinked. "Why are you here, Aleck?"

"I came to check up on you and see how you're doing." He took a step toward her.

When he reached out to touch her chin to tilt her head, her breath caught and it wasn't from the pain.

"That looks bloody awful. What is that? Six staples?"

"Eight," she whispered.

"I'm sorry." He shook his head. "So damn sorry that bastart hurt you too while trying to get to Kenzie."

"I'm all right. We both are."

"Aye, thank God. I came to thank you too."

"Thank me?" Why was he still lightly holding her chin?

"For texting me. If you hadn't, things could've ended quite a bit for the worse."

She lifted her gaze and knew it was a bad idea. Her gaze locked on his and something shifted inside her. Grew warm.

"I knew you'd come," she finally said softly.

He traced the edge of her jaw with his thumb, moved in

slightly toward her mouth.

Her heart sped up and without intending to, she leaned forward, lifting herself up onto her tiptoes. Her lips brushed his.

He went completely still, before he cursed against her mouth and moved his lips against hers. His tongue delved deep, teasing and stroking. Tasting her as much as she did him.

And just as quickly as it started, it was over. He pulled away, his gaze wide with disbelief.

"Shit, I'm so sorry," she muttered, her body starting to shake with shock. "It's the pain meds—they're pretty strong and make me a little loopy. Can we forget that just happened?"

What had she done? What had she *done*?

"It's forgotten already." He turned to stride toward the door. "See you on Friday, and not a day earlier."

"But I work tomorrow."

"If you come in, I'll simply send you home. Get yourself healed, Delonna. I'll make sure you still get paid."

He disappeared a moment later, and she leaned back against the wall with a ragged sigh.

So, yeah, that had just happened. She'd kissed her boss. *Fuck.*

Walking into the kitchen, she glanced down at the bottle of prescription pain pills she had yet to touch.

What in the everlasting hell had she been thinking?

The End

The McLaughlins

Book 1: *One More Round*
Ian McLaughlin's story

Book 2: *Straight, No Chaser*
Colin McLaughlin's story

Book 3: *Top Shelf*
Kenzie McLaughlin's story

Book 4: *Last Call*
Aleck McLaughlin's story

Available now at your favorite online retailer!

About the Author

Shelli is a New York Times and USA Today Bestselling Author who read her first romance novel when she snatched it off her mother's bookshelf at the age of eleven. One taste and she was forever hooked. It wasn't until many years later that she decided to pursue writing stories of her own. By then she acknowledged the voices in her head didn't make her crazy, they made her a writer.

Shelli is a true pluviophile (lover of rain) and currently lives in the Pacific Northwest with her husband and two daughters. She writes various genres of romance, but is most known for her contemporary series such as Holding Out for a Hero, The McLaughlins, and A is for Alpha. She's a compulsive volunteer, and has been known to spontaneously burst into song.

Visit her website at ShelliStevens.com.

Thank you for reading

Top Shelf

If you enjoyed this book, you can find more from all our great authors at TulePublishing.com, or from your favorite online retailer.

TULE
PUBLISHING

Made in the USA
Monee, IL
27 March 2022

93630064R00156